One For The Team
A Happy Holiday Short
Aria Daze

Contents

Content Warnings

This book contains themes that may be distressing to some readers. Please review the following information before diving in. Your mental health matters!

- Sexual activity

- Manipulation (Not between MC's)

- Cursing

- Alcohol use

- Slang (Yes, them folks be using ebonics. Please do not email me about it.)

- Group sex including but not limited to: Double penetration, Double vaginal penetration, Lucky Pierre's, Airtight Gangbangs.

- Privacy invasion

If this is your jam, please continue onward, dear reader! If not, please consider checking out other books in my catalog. **This book is not recommended for anyone under 18 years of age!**

Dedicated to all my queer readers. I love y'all to the moon and back.

And to good girls who love bad books.

Chapter 1

Genesis

Chrissy

I pretend to be ok, but deep down I want a group of oiled up black and brown men to run a train on me.

I know what you're thinking, "*Girl, what the fuck?*"

Trust me, it's a question I've asked myself a few times. Monogamy is in. My Instagram feed is full of photogenic duos posting curated vacation shots with the hashtag #couplegoals. My parents and grandparents have been married over 60 years combined, and here I am thinking about taking two dicks at once.

Or three.

Or four.

Five would be a bit excessive though.

The point is, I'm a grown adult, and if I want to have a handful of boyfriends at my beck and call, I should be able to. Who decided that one is the golden number?

"Chrissy, we need to talk."

Talk? Apparently one isn't all that great either.

My work pack slid to my feet right along with my jaw. It's not like me and Derek had been dating long, but I thought things were going well. We just had a movie night and celebrated our one year mark with a shared cheesecake. What happened?

"Um, about what?" I mumbled.

"Listen, I think you're great," Derek started.

Great? What's next? It's not you it's me? How long had been planning this?

"It's really not even you, it's me."

God, niggas are so predictable. It's almost embarrassing at this point.

"Get to the point," I hissed.

That snapped him out of his sorrowful charade immediately and his shoulders squared with previously suppressed irritation.

"Well this is part of it!" he clicked. "You're always so..."

"Direct?" I finished.

"Unladylike!"

"So I'm unladylike because I don't believe in beating around the bush?"

Derek scrubbed a hand down his face and it was almost like he had wiped away my attraction to him. I wasn't sure how I ended up here, standing in my living room with a man that should've never made it past casual drinks, but maybe it was loneliness. A quick lapse in my judgement. Twelve months wasn't a terribly long time, but I realized I could've been passing my days with someone better. Someone less ostracizing, that's for sure.

"You're unladylike because you're basically a glorified stripper!"

"I'm quite literally the opposite. I'm a professional mascot. Do you even know what I do for a living?" I sighed.

"I know you entertain other men by dancing for a living. That's pretty on par with the definition of a stripper," he argued.

"I thought this was implied by the name, but clearly not. So let me clarify something for you. To be a stripper, you have to STRIP! I'm in a 30 pound rabbit costume twice a week!"

Technically it was a hare, but I was highly doubtful that Derek knew what that was. Hell, he didn't even know what a stripper was.

"So you don't be twerking?"

"Sometimes, but since when do you not like women throwing ass?"

I'd seen his Instagram bookmarks. Every single one of those posts made me want to queue up Say It Like That by Sza on the speakers. Cause I was sensitive about having no booty.

"I don't like it when it's my woman! You know my family is Pentecostal. How am I supposed to explain your "profession" to my mom's and them? "

See. That's what I didn't like. You meet someone, you tell them about yourself, and they pretend to be all about it until you get in a relationship. Then they tell you should change because your life makes someone who you're not even fucking uncomfortable. That wasn't my issue.
"Since my job is such a big problem, I'll make it easy for you," I smiled.
I didn't miss the look of relief on Derek's face when I said that. Poor baby didn't even know what was coming.
"You can let your mom's and them know we're no longer together, and make sure you mention that you'll be moving back home. I don't want my stripper ways to corrupt your Christian life."
He was wearing mixed cloth, eating shellfish, and shacking up, but it was my career that was the problem. Yeah ok.

"Now Chrissy, baby. You know I didn't mean it like that," Derek said, trying to backtrack.
"No, I think you did," I shrugged, picking up my pack. "Anyway, I got to get to my job, where they pay me handsomely."
It was a low blow considering Derek's modest salary, but he took it there first.
"We'll talk about this when you get off," he said, withholding the ire in his tone.
"No we won't," I scoffed. "Start packing your shit. I'm

taking you off the lease Monday."

I heard him yell my name as I slammed the door but that belligerent buffoon no longer had any hold on me. This was my life to live. Not his or his Mama's.

"Girl, he called you a stripper? Does he know what a stripper is?" Milly asked, her wheezing laughter rippling through my car's speaker.

I was on the way to work but I still did what every black girl does after a breakup. I called my cousin and talked shit about dude. A tradition was a tradition.

"Honestly I don't know and I don't care. Derek isn't my problem anymore. I'm officially single," I shrugged.

"About damn time!" Milly cheered.

It was no secret that Milly did not care for my relationship with Derek. When I first introduced them and asked her what she thought several days later she just said, *"If you like it, I love it."* Which we all know is code for, *"That man is trash."*

And he was.

"Hopefully now you'll take Blessing's fine ass up on his **several** offers to be your man," Milly giggled.

Lord, not this again. I knew she'd bring this up, but who could blame her?

Blessing Harrell was the Minneapolis Hare's beloved center and the league's 2024 player of the year. He was 29, six foot one, and 225 pounds of lean muscle wrapped in skin so deep it almost sparkled under the stadium lights. He was objectively handsome in a real, "I'd ride his face until the New Year," kind of way. On top of being unfairly wealthy, extensively educated, and enviously kind. Obviously, he was Minnesota's most eligible bachelor. Which is why I felt inclined to tell Milly that he was **not** trying to be my man.

The reason she believed otherwise is simply because sometimes we ate our pregame together and he often extended me invitations to hang out with him and a couple of the other guys on the team. I think he was just being friendly since I was technically still kind of new with my year anniversary coming up just next week. So I often declined because of that. I didn't want to intrude on their dynamic just because he felt sorry for me, plus it used to make Derek uncomfortable.

He also swore up and down that Blessing was trying to get at me.

But me and Blessing were just friends.

Friends. Friends. Friends.

"That man does not want me," I laughed. "Anyway I gotta go. I just pulled up."

"Mhm, have a good game. Make sure you tell Blessing you're single now! Love you cousin."

"Goodbye with your messy ass," I scoffed before adding, "I love you too."

I loved Milly to death but she did not know what she was talking about. Minnesota's finest was not interested in me like that.

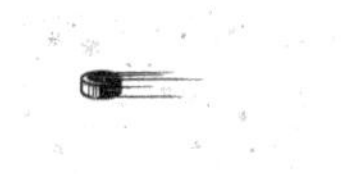

Blessing

It was freezing out so the crowds weren't too heavy and it was one of the rare instances during a northern winter where the roads were clearer than vodka. But she still wasn't here. She was late and Chrissy was almost never late. I hoped everything was ok. Mostly because I knew I couldn't step in and fix it. As much as I wanted to. As much as I wanted her.

When management told us our new mascot was a woman, I just knew they were going to bring in some bimbo who was all body and no talent to shake her ass in a tiny costume and boost viewership. Instead what we got was Chrissy Hawkins, a Juilliard graduate with an extensive resume and some serious athletic ability. Her dance moves did boost viewership, but it's because somehow she still found the energy to engage the crowd while lugging around that hot ass suit. She could hit a split on the ice and then hop up and high-five kids passing by in the stands. While I was the official face of the team along with Bear, Davis, and Little Foot, she was the heart of it.

She was also fine as hell with a face like an angel, but much to my dismay, she had a boyfriend. A boyfriend that she was loyal to, unfortunately. Chrissy would always try to talk, Desmond, or whatever his name was, up to me when we did our pregame catch up, but I was never impressed. He had a little bank account, no car, no ambition, and a whole lot of attitude. Always telling her what she could and couldn't do. Then one time he borrowed her shit and forgot to pick her up from work. My daddy would call him a buster, but I'm not that well-mannered. He was a bitch in my eyes.

Chrissy deserved better, and I'd been trying to tell and or show her that for the last year, but I never had any luck. Hopefully that would change today though. Our bye week began tomorrow night and I planned to use that brief break to convince her to spend some time together. Without the company of her so-called boyfriend.

"Bless, they're calling for us. Come on," Little Foot sighed.

The game was starting in just thirty minutes and we needed to stretch, but I wanted to see her first. Even if she wasn't technically mine, she was still my good luck charm.

"Just tell them I'm taking a shit or something. I need like three more minutes."

"Bless, she's probably running late."

"She never runs late," I argued.

"Never say never."

I knew Thaxton was probably right. Chrissy was likely running late, but something told me if I waited just a little longer I could find out why. And just before L could drag me off to the locker rooms, Chrissy came bounding in.

Her coffee-hued skin shimmered under the dim fluorescent lights like the manifestation of magic. Her hips swayed with each quick stride, encouraging her freshly braided hair to swish against her back, and her nutmeg brown eyes glowed with new determination. She was so determined that she almost breezed right past me. But I stopped her with a gentle tap on the shoulder before she could get too far.

"Hey, Chrissy," I beamed warmly, interrupting her dark cloud.

"Hey, Bless. I'm sorry I didn't see you at first. I'm just kind of in my own head."

I could tell. She looked irritated. Angry even.

"Is everything ok?" I asked.

Please say no. Please say no. Please say no.

"It's nothing," she sighed.

Damn, so much for hope.

"I just broke up with my boyfriend."

HALLELUJAH! How often is God good? You better answer all the time! I prayed for that niggas downfall everyday and I almost broke into a full praise dance hearing that it had finally happened. Won't he do it!

"Oh no," I said, bringing my hand to my mouth to feign distress. "What happened?"

"We just got into a disagreement about my job," she pouted, poking that cute bottom lip out.

"Why? Did he think something's going on between us?"

I hope he did. While the other two were respectful, I didn't try to hide the way I felt about Chrissy. I wanted him to know this wasn't the place to get comfortable. His girl worked for the NHL and niggas were creeping. Myself and my boys included.

"He always thinks that. But no, I've told him that we're just friends," she laughed, waving a pretty manicured hand in dismissal.

Friends?

No.

I didn't want to suck a fart out of my friend's asshole. I didn't hold games up for friends. I didn't get jealous and want to give my friends the whole wide world and everything in it.

"I'm not your friend, Chrissy," I said firmly, letting my eyes drag over her soft body.

Her expression told me she was distraught over my admission but her body language said something different. Her bottom lip puckered with a questioning pout, while her ample chest poked out ever so slightly, inviting me to step closer. I wasn't one to turn down an invitation so I moved close enough to smell the sweet cocoa butter lingering on her skin. She smelled better than I imagined she would. Which is crazy considering her scent reminded me of the bougie ass bakery in Downtown East. But that was just the magic of Chrissy Hawkins.

"Wait, what?" she squeaked, finally realizing what I said.

"I'm. Not. Your. Friend," I repeated, tipping her chin upward so I could stare into her eyes.

Chrissy leaned forward slightly as if she wanted to press

her lips against mine, but she hesitated for just a millisecond too long.

"HARRELL! Get your ass to the locker rooms now!" Coach hollered, interrupting the moment.

I was already on thin ice for ditching our last presser, so I knew I couldn't push it any more than I had. But rest assured this wasn't the end of our conversation. Chrissy was single and I was fresh off of Christmas break and about to go into another one. I had all the time in the world, and I was about to use every second of it pursuing her.

Emery (Ox)

"Bless man, where the fuck were you at? Coach was about to put us on drills next week," I hissed.

"He was bothering Chrissy again," Little Foot mumbled.

"Nigga, leave that lady the fuck alone before she reports you! She has a boyfriend," I chided.

"Not anymore," Blessing smiled slyly.

Not anymore. The words rang in my mind like an alarm. Repeating constantly.

"Wait, they broke up?" I gasped.

Bless nodded and my eyes immediately shot across the ice to where our mascot was standing. You'd never know it based on that suit, but Chrissy had body for days. Big titties, big thighs, curvy hips. She was lacking a little in the ass department but no one gave a fuck because her face was so pretty that she could give Aphrodite a run for her money. Siren eyes with a seductive rum color, high cheekbones, an arrow shaped nose that reminded me of the sculptures of ancient orisha, and a perfect pair of rounded lips. Chrissy was bad as fuck.

Half the team had a crush on Chrissy and that included some of the married guys. I couldn't blame them though. It was hard not to like her. Luckily divorce was costly in the league so they'd likely never act on it. Plus as personable as Chrissy was, she was still very guarded. Blessing asked her to hang out with the three of us once a month and she was yet to accept. Hopefully I could change that some time soon though.

"Shit, it's my time to shine," Little Foot laughed.

"What the hell do you mean, your time to shine? She's never even spoken two words to you," Blessing scoffed.

"Yes she has. She wished me happy birthday a few months back," L argued. "Plus she seemed to like what she saw when I was doing my stretches."

That lady was minding her business while facing the opposite direction. Thaxton was delusional. But not more so than I.

"Have y'all ever stopped to think that she might not want either one of you? A woman like that don't need a puppy, she need a big dawg."

"Don't you start!" Blessing hissed. "I was here first."

I understand where Blessing was coming from. He'd been waiting on Chrissy to become available since he met her. But I had to check him on that shit because none of that mattered if she wasn't feeling him. Hell, if she wasn't feeling any of us.

"She's a woman, not a playground slide," I scoffed. "It doesn't matter who was here first. At the end of the day, she picks who's next."

"Yeah, you're right," they conceded.

"And it's gonna be me," I smiled. "Thanks for playing."

"Man, what the fuck? That's that bullshit," and, "Shut up, Ox," followed.

But I was serious. If Chrissy was leaving with anyone tonight, I wanted it to be me. I was David Ruffin, and these niggas were The Temptations.

"Aight, how about this," L started. "Whoever shoots the most goals tonight gets the girl."

"Why would you say that? You know Bless is center, right?" I groaned.

"Yeah, but he ain't the only one with a stick. Whoever shoots the most shoots their shot. And the other two take a seat. Deal?"

"Fine," I grumbled.

"Deal," Bless smiled.

Chrissy

I'm biased, I know, but either way the Minnesota Hare's are the best team in the league. Last season we ended 79-3 and the losses were mostly because Ox was sick that week. We were good on the regular, but the guys were straight beasts tonight. It's like Christmas break gave them new wings or something. That or everybody was juicing.

I almost felt bad for the Indiana Hawks because they were getting steamrolled out there. Their goalie was getting pounded so bad you'd think there were four pucks on the ice. It seemed like Little Foot and Blessing were knocking their dreams into the net while Ox was busy sending men into orbit.

I hyped up the crowd when the commentators announced Blessing's third goal of the second quarter, and his 5th all night. Bodies rolled on my command, creating a sea showcasing our white, black, and Arctic blue jerseys. Then right as hands began to drop on the right side, I fell into a spinning split. Skates scraped against the ice aggressively while the crowd went wild. We were almost to the halfway point in the season and I think this was the best game the guys ever played.

I'm glad they found their mojo.

Sometimes I'm required to be at the pressers if the game is uneventful, but not tonight. The reporters had plenty to talk about from the match. So as soon as the crowd filed out, I snuck off to the showers. Everyone assumes that I'm freezing my ass off at work because of the ice, but that couldn't be further from the truth. I'm a hot, sweaty mess after lugging around a thirty-pound suit for 90 minutes. Which is why I appreciate an opportunity to thoroughly degrease my swamp ass. But this time I stayed so long that the facility guys started turning the lights off.

Message received.

I ain't have to go home but I had to go somewhere.

Going somewhere was the tricky part though. I didn't want to go home for obvious reasons, and while I loved Milly, I knew I wouldn't be able to stand witnessing her perfect little marriage right now. It was my parent's date night, so that was an obvious no if I didn't wanna hear my papa singing Teddy Pendergrass while he violated my mama, and my best friend Vance was on a baecation in the Maldives since he had finally bagged him a rich one. That left two options, a late night bar or a hotel. Or if I was feeling frisky, a combination of both. But first I needed to leave the stadium and find something to eat. I'm glad the guys had a good game, but matching their energy ran me ragged.

I fully expected to be one of the only people left in the building, but when I got to the lobby Blessing, Ox, and Little Foot were standing there chatting. Blessing looked good in his postgame compression fit, of course, but so did Little Foot, and so did Ox. All three of them were over six feet, and while Ox was the biggest, it's not like the other two were small change. While Ox towered over everyone with wide shoulders, strong forearms to match, a thick midsection, and two Christmas hams for an ass, Thaxton was willowy with an impressive wingspan, a tight core, and some of the nicest thighs I'd ever seen in my life. I stood there watching their taut, muscular bodies ripple underneath their sweatpants and thermals for at least two minutes before I realized they were staring back *and* smiling.

If only they knew what I was thinking.
ALL ABOARD!

"Hey, Chrissy. You did great tonight," Ox exclaimed sweetly.
"Oh, thank you," I said, feeling warmth flood my face. "So did you. I really liked your defensive roundabout in the third quarter."
It was a great play that surprised even the coaches. I'd probably watch that back for years to come. I had more to talk about, but Ox blushed like a rose in the background while Little Foot stepped forward.
"The whole team was talking about your kick split. Half of us probably would've fallen on our ass trying something like that," he added.
"Psh," I scoffed. "I doubt it. You guys played a great game. I was just matching energy."
The guys all exchanged a smile.

"Speaking of matching energy," Bless started. "We were going to get dinner to celebrate. You should come."
I almost said yes simply due to the fact that I was starving, but Ox and Little Foot stepped back with small frowns. I didn't know what was going on, but they didn't seem super excited that Blessing was asking me along. Plus I hadn't forgotten what Blessing said before the game. Maybe they knew something I didn't.
"Are you sure?" I asked and all three of their shoulders slumped.
Something told me they were disappointed. Something urgent.

"Listen, I know I keep declining, but I really don't want to intrude," I explained.

"You're never intruding, Chrissy," Little Foot laughed. "Come with us."

"Yeah," Ox nodded. "We'd love to spend more time with you. You're a part of our team."

"See? Not intruding," Bless smiled.

All three of them hit me with charming, pearly smiles and I almost melted into the tile on the spot. I guess maybe I had misread their expressions earlier. Plus I was pretty hungry.

"Well, ok," I nodded. "Just let me get my car."

"Nah no need, princess. You can just ride with us in the Escalade," Ox interjected. "Carpooling saves the planet." He did have a point and who was I to turn down luxury leather seating and a chance to ride on- I mean with Emery Greene? Maybe this was the universe closing a door and opening a window.

"That's fine by me," I smiled.

Chapter 2

Let Them Eat Cake

Little Foot

Ox thought he was slick, but I had to hand it to him, he kinda was. He had me and Bless sulking in the back seat while Chrissy rode with him up front. She wanted to compare features in her car and his since she also had a Cadillac, and Ox ate that shit up. "Can we pick a different song?" Bless grumbled.

It took all my willpower not to laugh in his face when he folded his arms over his chest like a toddler who'd been told no.

"What!? You don't like Ravyn Lenae?" Chrissy shrieked.

"He has terrible taste in music," Ox laughed while skipping around in the playlist.

We finally landed on Roc Steady by Megan Thee Stallion which seemed to satisfy everyone. Especially Chrissy. Damn, she could dance. Those hips and legs just didn't quit.

"I love Ravyn, but her voice makes me sleepy sometimes. It's too much excitement going on for all of that," Blessing clarified.

Chrissy rolled her body along to the reverb of the bridge and Ox almost scraped a curb trying to look at her.

There was excitement alright.

"Nah I understand that. I can't listen to too much Syd sometimes for the same reason," Chrissy offered.

"You like Syd? She's having a show in Chicago next month," I interjected.

"I know, I've been thinking about going but I'm not sure if I can swing the tickets and the hotel so soon after the holidays," she sighed. "I'm trying to save for a house."

"I get that. Hey if you want you can go with me, I got an extra ticket and I always book a suite when I stay somewhere overnight."

Did I have an extra ticket? No. But was I swiping my phone open furiously fast to get one? Absofuckinglutely. I needed a contingency plan. Bless won tonight, not all of winter.

Speaking of Blessing, he was staring at me like he wanted to punch my teeth out.

"Think fast, hoe," I mouthed with a smile.

"Maybe I'll tag along with y'all and we can make it a mini-team outing," Bless called, keeping his eyes on me.

"Yeah, that sounds fun," Ox agreed.

My expression dropped immediately. So much for contingencies.

"Look at them, wanna hang with us," I chuckled. "Don't worry, we'll ditch them and go shopping or something."

Ox and Blessing's frowns mirrored each other. I knew that neither one of them liked to shop, and they knew I was playing dirty. So it didn't surprise me when Blessing sent me a text.

> Nigga I hate you.

> You didn't hate this dick the other day now did you?

> Since you think you know everything. You got your fucking degree.

> That shit was MID

> Keep talking. Bottoms come a dime a dozen. I'll find a new one.

> You don't mean that. ⊠

Did I mean that?

Eh.

Don't get me wrong, I loved Blessing, but I needed Chrissy. Clearly he understood because he was in the same type of bullshit. All three of us were going tit for tat like we didn't have to go back to the same house tonight. But that was because Chrissy was gold personified. She was funny, thoughtful, and headstrong and all those qualities plus more were evident in every interaction. From the way she interacted with the whole team, to the effort she put forth when it was one of our birthdays, and even the way she spoke to our friends and family when they came to games. Chrissy Hawkins was something special.

Chrissy

The guys suggested a steakhouse: A local joint that sat off the river, and I was all for it. Especially after I looked up the menu. They had every cut of meat you could ask for as well as some prime seafood. Steak Oscar with a side of scallops? Yes please. It was a bit pricier than what I was used to to be honest, but I figured I was hanging with the big dogs so it was fine. I would just eat small and enjoy their company.

Speaking of their company, the boys had been absolute gentlemen the whole night. They fought over opening my door, helping me out, and even pushing in my chair at dinner. Blessing continuously offered me bites off his plate when I expressed interest, and Ox kept my glass full. It was cute. I didn't know why I didn't do this with them sooner.

Actually I did.

Derek's lame ass.

Tsh.

"That was good," Ox said while stacking our plates. "But now I need something sweet."

"Me too," Little Foot sighed. "I'm gonna order dessert. Chrissy, do you want anything special?"

I had taken a peek at the dessert menu and their prices matched the ambience in this place.

Rich and elevated.

Those water candles and leather booths had to come from somewhere so I wasn't mad at it, but dinner would definitely push me over my modest $120 budget.

"I actually hit my cap, so I'm good," I smiled.

"Cap?" Blessing queried.

"Uh, well yeah. Like my budget," I explained.

"Wait, who told you that you had a budget?" Ox questioned.

"Oh, I didn't want to assume. So I just planned to pay for myself. It's no big deal, really."

All three of them looked offended, but when they exchanged glances, I could swear Blessing was almost telling them I told you so. I had a feeling they had this conversation before.

"Is everything ok?" I asked, feeling restless in my once-comfortable chair.

I shuffled, causing three pairs of eyes focused on me with the intensity of a diamond drill. Listen, I'm not new to this, I'm true to this. At 30 years old I had been around the block enough times to know what that look meant. They wanted to fuck me. All three of them.

And unfortunately I wasn't opposed.

"Mamas, you don't have a budget when it comes to us. You can have whatever you want. We're not taking hockey sticks to the ankles just for fun," Little Foot explained.

"Exactly that," Ox co-signed.

"So what will it be?" Bless smiled with eyes that sparkled. "Dessert here or to go?"

You know when you read romance novels and the FMC always plays cute and humble and refuses to spend any of the MMC's money? Yeah, I hated that shit. They were offering and I was partaking. My budget didn't speak humble. The only thing I wanted out of the mud was potatoes.

"I'll take some chocolate cake and another glass of Merlot," I purred.

"You got it," they said in unison.

Ox took that request as an opportunity to order a bottle and an entire chocolate cake for the table, but I wasn't complaining. The wine loosened me up and allowed me to enjoy the unlikely but fun possibility of my ending up in a compromising position between all three of the guys, while the chocolate cake eased us into an easy conversation about life.

"You know I didn't start liking chocolate cake until college?" I admitted.

"What? How is that possible?" Little Foot exclaimed.

Don't get me wrong, I know that's a preposterous statement, but it was the truth.

"Listen, my experience with cake was mostly the dollar store box mix my Mama would whip up. For some reason the chocolate kind was always dry as fuck. So I just assumed that chocolate cake was dry," I shrugged. "Until I went off to school and got a meal plan. There was this lady named Gertrude who worked the cafeteria during late shift. She was mean as fuck but that cake? It made me understand addictive personalities."

"I'm glad you came over to the right side," Blessing chuckled while feeding me the last bite.

I knew it wasn't right but I couldn't help myself. I kept my eyes on Blessing while I licked the fork clean. My hands remained planted on the table while my tongue slowly eased up the delicate tines to collect the residual chocolate. Of course Blessing was staring but I didn't miss Emery and Thaxton's expressions either. Emery bit his bottom lip while Thaxton held his breath. All three of them looked hot and bothered and just the thought of them finding their relief with and inside of me had my nipples pebbling.

"So, what was it like going to Julliard?" Ox asked, smoothing the tension.

I knew he was just trying to change the subject to lighten his and the guy's mental load, but I was still excited. No one ever asked me about my college days before and it was one of the best times of my life. As sad as that previous revelation was, I launched into a story about how I once wholeheartedly believed I'd become a Rockette.

"Listen," I started. "So when I first got in..."

The waitress quietly slipped our bill onto the table beside us to avoid interrupting my story. We'd been at dinner for four hours and I was beyond happy I had come because it kept me from thinking about home. Plus I was learning so much about the guys. Like how Thaxton baked on the weekends. Then how Ox wanted to be a figure skater but was pushed into hockey because of his overwhelmingly large stature.

"You still skate beautifully out there," I said, rubbing his arm.

"A compliment from Miss split kick herself? This really is my lucky night," he chuckled.

"Honestly. I'm jealous of the crowd," Bless sighed. "I'd love to see that split up close."

"Cosign," Little Foot added with a two finger salute.

Ok yeah, they were definitely trying to fuck me. This was fun but I couldn't let it continue. I'd spend the next month sexually frustrated and dreaming about what ifs. I didn't need that kind of distraction. I was going to end up drooling over Thaxton's stretches again. That costume was hard to clean.

"Listen, guys. I can read subtext. You obviously find me attractive, and I definitely find you attractive. But I'm gonna have to rain on this parade. No sane person could possibly pick between you all, so this ends here."

The table went quiet, and then they exchanged that secret look again.

"You know, you assume a lot, Chrissy," Thaxton chuckled.

"Excuse me?" I balked, bringing my hand to my chest.

"You're excused, darling. But L is right. You assumed about dinner and you're assuming now," Blessing sighed. "What did I assume? Were you or were you not being sexually suggestive over a split five seconds ago?"

"Oh, no I was. You're right, you're great at reading subtext because I definitely meant I'd love to see that split up close on my dick," Blessing chuckled. "But nobody mentioned you having to choose."

Blood rushed south, pulling the air out of my lungs with it. I was certain I wasn't hearing him right. Maybe I was having a stroke. Or maybe I got hit with a puck on the ice earlier and I was now in a coma dream. Either way I needed him to repeat that.

"What?" I gasped, feeling faint.

Ox peeled a few hundreds off the knot in his wallet and paid the bill while the other two grew closer. Blessing swallowed the last of his drink before his darkened gaze aligned with mine. He didn't bother to look away or clarify anything as Thaxton nibbled my ear.

"The only choosing you're doing tonight is picking what position you wanna be fucked in, Mamas. We're down for whatever you wanna do," Thaxton whispered against the curve of my neck.

I was hearing them, but I wasn't really hearing them. I was still convinced that somehow I had forgotten English and this was all one big mistranslation.

"You wanna share?" I gulped.

"We already share a house, bills, and a profession," Ox

laughed. "We like each other enough to share a lover as wonderful as you."

Blessing kissed me while Ox and Little Foot kneaded my tits and thighs. Their touches were all so different but they worked in perfect harmony. I wondered how their strokes would sync.

"How does this work?" I gasped.

"How does what work?" Thaxton gruffed.

"Sex," I mumbled in a small voice. "Sex between the four of us."

"Easy," Blessing laughed. "Ox is heteroflexible. He doesn't do penetration, but he does enjoy frotting and sucking. I'm a bi verse and Thaxton's a pan top. We all get tested once a month and we're clean. We got the paperwork to prove it. So you got plenty of options for tonight. Rubbers, Raw, on the hood of the Escalade. Whatever you want to do, we can do it."

Well that was a thorough explanation. Clearly they had thought this out before.

"How many times have you done this?" I hissed as Emery's fingers trailed the sensitive skin of my belly underneath my shirt. "Never. We rarely have the same taste in women, but then we met you. There's a first time for everything," Thaxton explained.

There was indeed a first time for everything. Because this was the first time three fine-ass men were offering to do whatever I wanted done. This was the first time I could possibly get my fantasy fulfilled.

Wait, why the fuck was I hesitating?

"Ok," I sighed with an agreeing nod. "I'm ready now."

"I promise we'll make it worth your time," Emery said with a bright, disarming smile.

Despite his grin, I didn't doubt it for one second, which is why I followed them clear out that door into the lion's den.

On the ride back to their place, I was handed multiple devices showing the guy's recent STD screenings. They were all clear and so was I, plus I believed in the baby-busting magic of IUDs. I was looking forward to getting railed with confidence, but I got side tracked by the downtown New Year's display when we stopped. I was transformed into a moth, completely captivated by all the twinkling lights and gilded structures. The arboretum was especially alluring.

"You excited for 2025?" Thaxton asked while rubbing my back.

His hands were strong but his fingers were nimble and capable. His thumb and pointer finger slowly worked the knots out of my neck while he waited for my reply.

"Yes and no," I answered honestly.

"Why the juxtaposition?" Blessing replied.

I released a steadying breath as Ox's hand fell to my knee. His touch was respectful, but my body's reaction wasn't. I was trying to maintain conversation but the two of them were making it difficult.

"Well yes, because a new year is full of new opportunities. I wanna travel, experience everything I couldn't this year, and of course grow. But no, because of what happened in

November and also Derek."

"Who the fuck is Derek?" Ox scoffed.

Emery's face scrunched up with offense, making me chuckle.

"Sorry, I forgot I only told Blessing about him. Derek is my ex-boyfriend. We broke up today because he wanted me to quit my job."

"To be honest, I never remember dude's name. But it doesn't matter anyway. Fuck that boy," Blessing shrugged.

Ox agreed but Thaxton appeared stressed. Eyebrows tense and jaw tight.

"Is he causing you trouble, Mamas?" he inquired while rolling over my collar bones. "Cause if so, we can handle that."

"Not really," I said quietly. "I just have to put him out. I let him join my lease when he lost his job a few months ago."

"You're a saint," Ox laughed. "That nigga would've been homeless fucking with me. Especially considering he wanted you to quit your job. What he thought you wanted to be a bum with him?"

"Em, he got another one," I laughed.

"Yeah, but tell them how much he makes," Blessing interjected.

I swung around to fully face him in the back seat. I half expected him to utter an apology for being an instigator, but the charming smile he offered me was unremorseful.

"Blessing Harrell!" I gasped.

"Tell them," he urged while pinching his bottom lip underneath his sharp canine.

I wondered why Blessing was being so stubborn about Derek until I met his eyes. His eyes hadn't left me once the entire time, and when I met his pupils with mine, his brown eyes surged with desire. Knowing that he wanted me made the truth slip from my mouth with a whimper. "Mid 20kish," I offered.

"Chrissy," Ox admonished while sucking his teeth. "You deserve better than that, baby girl."

"It wasn't serious, Em," I said with a dismissing wave. "Plus money doesn't make a man in my eyes."

"Money may not make a man, but yours should definitely have some," Thaxton chuckled. "How else is supposed to compete with the dudes that would buy you the world and everything in it while worshiping the ground you walk on?"

Thaxton also offered me a smile, but unlike Blessing's, his offered no hint of humor. It was grave and alarming yet rich like velvet. I wanted to wrap myself in it.

"Well, that doesn't matter now," Blessing said as we eeked to a stop.

The engine came to a paced purr as we rested at the long light before the highway, gently rocking my body. I heard a familiar *click* sound and then my seat belt retracted into the door, deserting me. Before I could realize what was happening or protest, I was pulled out of my chair and into the back seats. My palms met cool leather first, then the warm skin of Minnesota's best center and winger.

"We're going to make up for lost time, Chrissy," Blessing cooed while sitting me in his lap. "Starting with giving you everything you deserve."

Blessing's mouth pressed into mine with dizzying intensity. My lungs expelled a desperate breath, my chest falling against his with the same urgency as heavy rain. His hands roamed over my body like a discovery probe. Focused and thorough. Especially when he ran his fingertips under the hem of my rising shirt. He traced the sensitive cavern of my navel before letting his fingertips tickle the apex of my hip. Blessing's touch was euphoric and everything felt ridiculously right. But then Thaxton joined in.

He was careful, which surprised me. He slid me into the space between his spread legs without breaking my kiss with Blessing, a true Master of repositioning. His steeled length pressed against my lower back while his fingertips traced my areolas through my bra.

"I like watching you kiss my boyfriend," he whispered against my neck.

I always sensed that there was something deeper than friendship between Thaxton and Blessing, but I never cared to investigate. That was their business, not the leagues. But the confirmation was pleasing to me regardless. They were a handsome couple.

"Oh, sorry," I giggled. "Is he yours?"

"For the past three years," Thaxton nodded.

"Well, do you mind if I borrow him?" I teased with a seductive smirk.

"We can share him, Mamas," he chuckled while kissing my neck. "Gentlemen share with pretty women."

Thaxton's hand started to slip into my waist band when a car behind us blew their horn. The sound was obnoxious, but it did its job because it prompted Emery to focus on the road instead of us in the back seat.

"Let's wait until we get home," Blessing laughed. "Ox is about to crash the car."

"Honestly I was about to pull over. But these seats won't let back far enough for Chrissy to sit on my face," he replied.

My cheeks tingled from the tempting vision of me riding that sweet giant's face against custom cognac leather seating and I had to remind myself to swallow before I drooled.

"Yeah, let's wait," I nodded. "I wouldn't want to distract anyone."

"Well it's too late for that," Thaxton laughed.

"Way too late," Blessing agreed while tracing the outline of my stiff nipple.

I let my mind run amok in the gutters for the duration of the drive. It was easy to think about fat dicks driving me crazy in partnership with kisses that lit my existence on fire for thirty minutes when fat dicks were pressed up against me. But that changed the second we pulled up to the house. Emery punched in a four digit code then drove us through the heavy engraved copper privacy gate surrounding the property. The house itself was a red-brick mansion on top of a steep incline that overlooked The Lake Of The Isles, and that view was complimented by a giant wrap-around patio. I surveyed the area and caught the fire pit in the center of the outdoor space, but I guess my awestruck expression made Thaxton chuckle.

"Don't worry. We'll make plenty of time to keep you warm by a fire," he said while caressing my arm.

"Co-sign," Blessing and Ox added.

The guy's house was huge, but somehow it wasn't egregious. Everyone had their own separate room and then there were four guest rooms. Individual living quarters were decorated according to personal taste while communal areas were filled with cozy neutrals, pastels, and lively greenery. Space was plentiful, but maximized and utilized efficiently. There weren't any big awkward areas of forgotten space like you see in most Mcmansions, and most importantly, it was spotless. The air carried the faint aroma of bleach and the ever-elusive orange Fabuloso. I knew they had a cleaning lady because she left Thaxton a recipe on the fridge from when she stopped by earlier that day, but I also saw Ox and Bless wiping down the surfaces as they put the leftover cake away and got beverages together. Which meant this was their standard.

"I love your house," I whispered. "I mean that genuinely."
"Thank you," the guys smiled. "We realized pretty quickly that we all had similar mindsets. We know we can't do this shit forever, so we wanted to be smart about money. There's no point in owning three of these big ass houses when we can all co-own one and split the bills, the maintenance, and the taxes three ways. There's enough space in here for a small village."
"That is smart," I agreed.
It was refreshing to hear about the guys thinking past hockey. I knew they loved the game, but it couldn't last forever. Eventually they'd have to call it and move on.

"This is also smart," Emery said while picking me up and placing me on the counter for easy access.
Being fat never bothered me, but I knew there was a strong possibility I'd spend my days only being able to be lifted up in prayer. Especially while dealing with Derek. But not anymore. I was trying to figure out how to tell them I wanted to get started, meanwhile Emery had hiked me up like I weighed no more than a 5lb bag of flour. They weren't lying when they said my job came with some of the best benefits in the country. I'm so glad I didn't go with Disney.

"Spread your legs for me, princess," Emery whispered.
I did what was asked of me and he removed my pants, running his thick fingers down my thighs with every pull.

Eventually he came back to the top of my thighs and kneaded generous, soft circles into the flesh there.

"Blessing was right," Ox sighed contently. "Your skin is soft."

"Don't creep her out," Blessing chided while hooking his fingers under the hem of my shirt. "She's going to think I'm a stalker or some shit."

I barely blinked and I was half-naked. Only my undergarments and some ironically high socks remained. These niggas were professionals in every capacity.

"Wait what's going on?" I chuckled as Thaxton unhooked my bra.

"Nothing," Little Foot laughed. "We're just used to talking about you amongst each other. Me and Ox respected the fact that you had a man so we kept our distance, but Blessing would always tell us how soft you are after he hugged you to make us jealous."

"Really?" I chuckled.

"Yeah, well it worked," Blessing shrugged.

"It sure did," Emery nodded while tracing my seam through my panties.

I was uncomfortably wet. My panties were clinging to me like a second skin, the seat so soaked it was almost see through. I wanted Em to take them off, but he hesitated until I touched the top of his hand to refocus him.

"Can I touch you like this?" he rasped with a lecherous gaze.

I nodded just as Thaxton took my left nipple into his mouth while Blessing sucked my right. I arched into the pleasure allowing them further access to my breasts. Neither one of them hesitated to massage the soft flesh surrounding my steeled nipples, and that made my pussy throb with need. Luckily though, Emery was on it.

He rolled my panties down to my ankles before kneeling in between them. Ox was 6 '7 and that height was hard to miss, but it didn't truly dawn on me how big he was until I saw his head between my legs. My thighs looked like backpack straps against his wide shoulders.
"You smell so good," he groaned while rubbing his nose in it.
A small whimper escaped me when his coarse beard rubbed the inside of my thighs. One that seemed to spur the boys on. Thaxton took one leg and Blessing took the other to open me up completely, all while keeping their mouths occupied. Emery joined the oral fixation club by sweeping his deft tongue over my inner lips before taking my bud into his mouth. His fingers probed my entrance and tight ass while he ate me. The other two men kneaded my thighs according to Emery's rhythm, and when Thaxton had his fill of my nipple, his mouth traveled to meet mine.

A lot of men I had the displeasure of experiencing were ass at tongue kissing. They just ejected it into your mouth and let it sit there like a dead fish.
Not sexy.
Thaxton, however, was plenty versed in what to do. His tongue slipped into my mouth and wrapped around mine like a silk scarf. His rhythm matched Emery's, and when

the both of them made me moan, he swallowed the pleading sound like it was a drink of water.

"You like it when Ox sucks that pretty pussy, darling?" Blessing whispered against my neck.

He too took his mouth off my nipple to cause terror elsewhere, but his thumb was still working overtime to wreak havoc on my system as was Little Foot's. I was seeing literally stars between all of it, and clearly, I was in no space to speak. But they weren't satisfied. Thaxton withdrew from our kiss with a frustrated sigh.

"Blessing asked you a question, Mamas. Do you like the way Ox sucks that fat pussy?"

I tried to go back for seconds but he placed his thumb against my bottom lip and held my gaze until I answered.

"I do," I moaned as my wetness pooled on the cool marble counter beneath me. "So much."

"I know, Mamas," he chuckled while spreading my lips for Ox. "You're making a mess everywhere."

The skin of my ass was damp with proof. Proof that furthered when Ox curled his fingers upward against my walls. Between his magic tongue, Blessing's soft kisses, and Thaxton's dirty words, it didn't take me long to unravel. An overwhelming fullness overtook me when I peaked, but I felt comfortable to let go fully and let the three of them see me fall apart. Which turned out to be a surprise for all of us.

"Looks like we got a squirter, boys," Emery said, flicking his tongue out to remove my stickiness from his lips.

You hear about squirters all the time but after so many mid orgasms you start to think that kind of release is the stuff of myths and legends. Never did I expect to be proved wrong on a kitchen counter of all places. I was struggling to catch my breath but I couldn't contain my shock.

"I've never done that before," I huffed.

"Again, there's a first time for everything," Blessing chuckled.

He slowly eased two fingers into my ass, occupying the tight space Emery once was. My pussy puckered because she wanted to be touched on the inside too, but Thaxton was on it before I could vocalize it.

"Fuck, you get so wet," he hissed while thumbing my still sensitive clit. "Such a perfect woman."

He sank two curled fingers inside me which felt so good it almost distracted me from the sound of Emery's zipper. But my brain wouldn't let me miss anything that important.

"You like what you see, princess?" Emery asked while stroking his dick.

I did.

Emery was high yellow like an unfrosted sugar cookie, but his dick was the same dreamy pecan brown color as Thaxton. It was also wrapped with veins that pulsed every time his hand slid down his branchesque shaft, and his head was deceptively average. Like it was attached to a slimmer member that wouldn't wreck your insides.

"Put it in my mouth please, Emmy?" I asked.

Ox smiled and repositioned me so that my back was fully against the counter. Blessing and Thaxton didn't seem to have any complaints since they now had more access to my holes, and I especially didn't complain when Emery's throbbing dick depressed my tongue and filled my watering mouth. I stacked my hands one on top of the other and worked them up and down his length while he fucked my throat. I didn't have any ass but that was ok because I also didn't have a gag reflex. So when Emery shut his eyes to concentrate on not cumming I hummed a tune against him like I was a first lady who didn't listen to worldly music.

"Jesus, Chrissy. Shit," he cursed.
He was fighting for his life while Blessing and Thaxton were switching. I watched Thaxton lick his fingers clean before inserting them into my ass while Blessing opted to kneel and lick me.
"Fuck you taste so good," he groaned.
"Doesn't she?" Emery and Thaxton agreed. "Like Christmas."
I couldn't put my two cents in since my mouth was stuffed, so I gave a wobbly thumbs up instead.

Emery's dick was so massive that I could practically feel it in my pussy. His precum leaked into my mouth in thick silky spurts as I sucked and slobbered on his swollen tip. Meanwhile Blessing's mouth was becoming increasingly active between my thighs. His tongue wagged against my bud like he was spreading the good news of God's kingdom. I think he was trying to make me squirt like Ox did but I didn't have enough time to reload. That didn't stop me from orgasming though,so I had his face looking like a white-iced Hunny bun.

"Damn," Thaxton hissed.

He cursed with conviction so I pulled away from Emery to see what all the fuss was about. He was stroking his picturesque dick in one hand while probing my ass with the other. Unlike Emery's, it was completely smooth and straight, but his head was huge. It kinda reminded me of the toadstool monster on the OG Mario games and I immediately wanted to kiss it.

"I need everyone to switch for me if that's alright," I purred.

The boys immediately abandoned their tasks, eager for my directions.

"That's more than alright," Blessing smiled.

"Ok," I whispered, sitting up onto my palms.

Three fine ass men with brick hard dicks stood directly in front of me, ready to do whatever I asked. I had basically won the lottery and hit the jackpot.

"I wanna ride Emery while Thaxton fucks me from the back and Blessing fucks my throat."

I bit my lip while waiting for their response. I'd been watching too much gay shit in my free time and I knew it. It seemed egregious in my head but it sounded just plain greedy out loud. Maybe Derek's bitch ass was right about my directness being unladylike. I half-expected to see doubt appear on their handsome faces but instead they just smiled.

"That's fine by us," they chuckled.

Emery slid onto the counter next to me, and with one quick motion, I was turned around and pulled into his lap. At that moment I had confirmation that God was a woman because there was no other reason for the perfection that was Emery Greene. I gripped his expansive shoulders as I rolled my hips forward, indulging in every wanton touch I could while he leaned closer to encourage me. When we locked eyes my body shivered with excitement, but I had to remind myself to breathe when he pressed himself towards my opening.

Fuck, he was big.

Everywhere.

"There you go, princess. Nice and slow," he cooed, easing me down his length.

His hands gripped my hips to keep me steady during my descent while Thaxton's thumb traced soft, coordinated circles on my spine. I became loopy as all my blood rushed south, and soon my front was pressed against Emery's with my nipples grazing the raised ink of his chest tattoo. Then our pelvises met completely with my knees resting against the chilly marble. I shuddered, trying to contain the strangled moan that nearly clawed from my throat. I tilted my hips upward slightly only to collapse against his chest again. Emery took mercy on me and repositioned my head onto his shoulder before pecking my temple like I was some precious angel instead of a convulsing whore.

"I got you baby girl," he whispered while stroking my

shoulder blades.

What a sweetheart.

I used to tell Derek his dick was big all the time, but I was a fucking liar and this proved it. I was already so full I couldn't think, and I was supposed to take two of these? The universe was making an example out of my greedy ass.

"Damn, that pussy looks good," Blessing cursed from his spot behind us.

He rubbed his fingertips across my hood, inciting my eager nerves.

"It's about to look even better," Little Foot said while wetting his lips. "Do you still want some more company, Mamas?"

"Yes," I whimpered as I twitched against Ox. "Come on."

"Hang tight," Thaxton whispered lowly.

As if I had any other choice.

With one leg slung over my hip and the other planted on the ground, Thaxton carefully pushed his tip into the sliver of remaining space in my pussy. His hands gripped the counter with sickening strength, seemingly almost buckling the stone beneath us, all so he could enter me slowly.

"Jesus, this was a terrible idea," Emery hissed as Thaxton's length slid against his.

The two of them hissed as Thaxton entered me halfway, their pleasure palpable in the warmth surging between us.

"I'm so glad you're on birth control because there's no

way either one of us could pull out," Ox continued.

The thought of my cat overflowing with their warm, thick release nearly had me cumming. But then again that could've just been from Blessing's pointer finger that was still rolling over my swollen clit. His nails were trimmed short which is how I knew the slight roughness I felt could be attributed to callouses he developed from the sport. Which for some reason made the restraint he displayed ten times better. So, yeah Blessing was definitely the reason.

"You got room for one more, baby?" Blessing asked while tugging his length.

His dick was hard and heavy like ancient ebony wood with a slight left curve and also wrapped in veins. His head was heavy, but it was even with the rest of his member. It was perfect to wrap my tongue around.

"Yes please, Daddy," I groaned.

I've never been the Daddy type because my Papa was very much an active and instrumental part of my life, but it just felt right this time. Especially once Ox slipped Blessing into my mouth and all of the guy's thrust synced. I was being completely dominated and I loved every second of it. I knew they were team players before, but now!? We were winning the Stanley Cup this year.

I was sure of it.

"Ooh fuck, Chrissy," Thaxton panted. "Why do you feel so good, Mamas?"

"Perfect ass pussy," Ox huffed. "This don't make any sense."

He withdrew as Thaxton entered me, both of them meeting somewhere in the middle for a few glorious seconds that sent me into a frenzy. Ox's hands supported my waist while Thaxton gripped my ass. Despite that delightful restraint I bucked my hips wildly hoping that someone would catch what I was throwing. And catch it they did. They caught it so well that my pleasure leaked out onto them and clung to my thighs and their bellies, making a creamy white mess of the green marble.

"Please don't stop," I cried, popping Blessing's dick from my mouth.

"Never," they said in unison.

A lie never sounded so sweet.

I gave Bless a few sloppy, slow pumps before sliding him so far down my throat that my nose rested against his belly. The sensation of being full in two out of three holes was making me dizzy but I couldn't stop. I could feel every time Ox and Little Foot's tips rubbed together and my clit was so hard that it had a separate pulse from the rest of me. They stretched me so good that I could cry, and in fact I did when my orgasm began to crest. Tears streamed down my face as Thaxton and Emery throbbed against me and each other, their heads becoming fat and warm. Blessing's thumb brushed my nipples while I swallowed him, and after taking it like a champ for the better part of twenty minutes, my pussy threw in the towel. My orgasm ripped through me like a cyclone, wreaking havoc on every cell in my body and wetting up the counter underneath us. I didn't realize I was digging into Ox's bicep until he came and his muscles tensed underneath me, while Thaxton's did the same on top. All of that pressure, heat, and weight sent me over the edge again and I came as Blessing's warm, salty load ran down my throat.

The Minnesota Hares had ruined me.

How was I ever supposed to go back to normal after this?

Blessing withdrew from my mouth and slumped against the kitchen floor, his dick still very much hard but his sack visibly empty.

"You ok?" I squeaked.

My voice came out rough because of my dry, overused throat and Blessing immediately hopped up from the floor and got me a glass of water.

"I should be asking you the same thing considering you got two D1 athletes camping inside you," he chuckled while tilting the cup towards my lips. "Drink slowly."

"What about me?" Thaxton faux-whined.

"Ain't nobody tripping off you, Otis," Ox chuckled, his laugh deep and boisterous.

The vibrations rippling from his body reminded me that he was still in me and I clenched around both of them involuntarily.

"Sensitive," Ox groaned as I wiggled against him. "L pull out."

"Why do I have to pull out?" Little Foot scoffed. "I like it in here."

"Because if I try to pull out I'm probably gonna nut on your stomach."

"Sexy," Thaxton laughed while rolling his hips back.

Our seal broke with an obnoxious pop and their warm cum rushed out of me. If I had my faculties I would've been embarrassed to be so messy, but number 3, 47, and 19 had fucked that out of me.

"I need a rag," I groaned as Emery exited.

He left behind an unexpected feeling of profound emptiness, and it upset my spirit to know that he couldn't live inside of me.

"Come on, princess. I'll run you a bath," Ox said while sitting up.

He cradled me against his welcoming chest before sliding off the counter but Thaxton stopped him with a flattened palm. He looked bothered by something. But I couldn't figure out what because I expected him to be blissed out like Blessing.

"Why do you get to carry Chrissy?" he frowned.

"Because we're going to my room," Ox said plainly.

"Your room?" Bless scoffed. They were really arguing over whose shower I was about to defile. I almost had to rub my eyes to make sure I was seeing things right. Maybe this is what all those stank looks I noticed over dinner were about.

"Guys!" I exclaimed. "This is easily solvable. We'll just take over a guest room."

Tension bled from everyone's shoulders including mine upon hearing a logical solution. While it was clear that the guys were better at sharing than most, they still had possessive inclinations. I'd have to keep that in mind if I ever got around to doing this again. For now I was just going to enjoy a nice shower and soak.

Chapter 3
We Have A Problem

Blessing

"You're staring at her."

I grew jealous as I watched the fluffy white suds trail her silky brown skin. I wanted to touch her that way too. She was sitting in the center of the second guest room's garden tub sipping a hot echinacea and ginger tea that Little Foot had made for her, and she twirled the ends of her braids around her pointer finger while she conversed with Ox who was showering the next wall over. She sighed and watching her chest rise from that breath was like watching the sun climb into the morning sky. L was right.

I was staring.

"So what?" I scoffed at Thaxton. "She's beautiful."

She locked eyes with us standing in the bathroom door at that exact moment, rendering both me and L speech and motionless. Eventually she looked away and I became aware of my own heartbeat, but Thaxton was still frozen in time. With his concentrated gaze focused on nothing outside Chrissy's dazzling smile.

"Now you're staring too," I whispered while nudging him.

"Shut Up," L gruffed. "I was just practicing active listening."

"Speaking of which, I can put your show on. Abbott's already booted up on my Hulu," he said, whisking into the bathroom.

It was actually booted up on *my* Hulu because Thaxton almost never watched TV but I let him have it.

I stood in the door quietly as he put her requested episode on, gathered her hair in a ponytail so it wouldn't get wet, then kissed the end of her nose. L was an asocial dickhead on his best days but here he was fawning over Chrissy after only a few hours. Ox was no better, and I was one to talk. I had hearts in my eyes every time she smiled. I was a few seconds away from calling my optometrist.

I initially prepared for this to be a one-time thing but now I wondered if that was even possible.

"We need to talk," I whispered as Thaxton met me at the door.

"About what?"

The shower door swung open in a fit of rolling white steam. Ox stood stepped out with a towel around his waist and one wrapped around his locs, and he too kissed the end of Chrissy's mode before exiting.

"That's what we need to talk about," I huffed.

"Talk about what?" Ox asked as he stepped out from the bathroom.

"Shhhhh!" I hissed, peeking around his big ass to see if Chrissy heard us.

Luckily she was completely engrossed in the TV, dead to the world around her.

"Listen," I started, guiding the guys into a corner.

Before I could finish voicing my concerns, Ox's phone chimed obnoxiously loud with a notification. It must've been urgent because he kept his phone on DND.

"Damn, hold that thought," he said while sliding into jogging pants and house shoes. "Courier's here."

"Courier?" L exclaimed as Ox slipped down the hall. "What did you order?"

"Beee right bacckkk!" Ox called in a sing-song voice.

We heard him sprinting back upstairs not even two minutes later. Then he burst in with two armfuls of varied shopping bags.

"What the hell is this?" Thaxton queried.

"Pj's for Chrissy. Also socks, slippers, lotion, and drawls," he shrugged. "Speaking of which, do y'all think she can fit these?"

In his hand were a pair of size 16 satin briefs that deviated from her current pair only by color. Ox's choice was baby pink while her old ones were sage green.
"Yes," Thaxton nodded with a dumb smile.
"Ok cool. I heard women aren't supposed to wear dark colored panties because the dye can irritate their intimate areas," Ox replied.
"That's mostly a myth," I sighed while sliding my hand down my face.
I heard a cap flip and suddenly the most intoxicating smell known to all of the Midwest filled the room.
"Damn what the fuck?" Thaxton exclaimed while sniffing the lotion. "Why does this kinda smell like her?"

The yellow and black bottle brought me back to the first day we all officially met her. When my hands dried out during practice because I forgot my gloves. I was stubborn about using a replacement because I didn't wanna mess up my energy and while most of the boys were judging, Chrissy understood. She said mojo was important. When we got done for the day she jogged over and gave me a big squirt of her lotion from a miniature version of the container Thaxton was holding. She laughed when she rubbed it across my knuckles while mentioning something about keeping me photo ready.
That was the day I went to sleep with my hands covering my nose and a smile covering my lips.

"Because it's her favorite lotion, and she layers it with other stuff," I grumbled. "Ox why do you know that?"

"I don't know," he shrugged while folding a few tops. "I guess it's just something I noticed about her. She's noticeable."

"She really is," Thaxton sighed while staring into the bathroom.

Ox gave him the my man look while patting him against the chest. Then their goofy asses started jigging to some silent tune. If I had to guess based on how they were swaying I'd say it was some neo-soul shit. Certified hairy coochie music.

"This is what I wanted to talk about!" I whisper-hissed.

"What now, nigga?" Ox frowned. "We can't dance?"

"Not when y'all are dancing about Chrissy. This is a problem!"

"Why?" L challenged.

"Because y'all like her!"

"NAWWWW!" They sarcastically exclaimed.

Mufuckas did not lie when they said sexuality is not a choice. Because there was no way I should have been even remotely attracted to either of these dumbasses when women existed. But unfortunately, here I was.

"You know what I mean!" I challenged, with an irritated wave. "This isn't just a regular crush and some sexual tension. You two are trying to pursue a romantic relationship with her."

"Because I bought her some lotion?" Ox scoffed.

He was trying to play it down, but I knew Emery better

than that. We'd been playing together for almost a decade and living together for half that time. I could tell when he was feeling something serious with a woman, and he was really feeling Chrissy.

"No, Ox. Because you wouldn't let her walk up the stairs on her own, carried her to the tub, and then bought her an entire nighttime wardrobe."

Emery's shoulders slumped slightly, conveying defeat while Thaxton laughed. He shouldn't have found anything funny considering he was in the same boat, but I guess he never learned that lesson since he was one of them kids who weren't scared of whoopings.

"And you," I said, pointing to Little Foot. "You bought her a last-minute concert ticket to an almost sold-out show and you started looking at realtors as soon as she was in the shower."

Now everyone was tense with defeat. Even me.

Chrissy was gorgeous, witty, and talented. That was a fact. But another fact of the matter was there were three of us and only one of her. And that wasn't a fair choice to ask her to make. She already told us she wouldn't over dinner.

"Ok, so we all like-like her. We're grown. We can be in a polycule or something. It's 2024, I see poly people all the time on them find-a-fuck apps," Thaxton shrugged.

Ox nodded in agreement while continuing to pull clothes out of the bags. He had literally bought every color of pajama he could think of with socks to match. It was insane.

"Absolutely not," I scoffed.

"Oh what? Now you're too good for us?" Ox laughed. "I'mma sexy mufucka and I get bread. And L? L's a strong seven."

"Aye fuck you," L laughed while pushing him in the chest. For a brief moment I let myself entertain a four-way intersection between all of us, but that quickly dissolved when my eyes focused on the hockey sticks mounted on the wall behind us.

"It's not that guys," I sighed. "A lot of poly couples follow the standard one trash-ass nigga to three mids and that's slightly more socially acceptable. But it's three of us to one woman plus we're all famous. Chrissy would be getting slaughtered in the media."

"You know, that's what PR teams are for," Thaxton replied. "We can protect her. Or we can just keep it on the low so it's not a problem to begin with."

"But what about with our families? How can we expect them not to accidentally tell someone over Sunday gossip? Then Ox's pop is not gonna understand. What about Chrissy's family?"

They both went quiet, their eyes simmering with contemplation. Then Ox threw a pack of socks at me.

"You ruin everything! Will you shut the fuck up sometimes?" he gritted.

"Is everything alright in here?" An airy, melodic voice asked.

One belonging to the one and only Chrissy Hawkins.

"Yes. everything's fine," Thaxton responded immediately. "We're just trying to decide how to spend our bye week."

"Ha," Chrissy snorted. "All I know is I wanna sleep in tomorrow."

She pulled her long braided hair into a loose bun while her ample chest heaved with a sigh.

"Well, I didn't think this through. I don't have any back-up clothes."

"Oh, not to worry. I got you a few things," Ox offered while holding out her new panties.

She reached her little hand out and grasped them with a sly yet appreciative smirk.

"Whew, thank you. Because otherwise I might have had to borrow a jersey and some socks from one of y'all," she chuckled.

Why God!? I wanted to fall to the floor in anguish. Chrissy could've been in a pair of thigh-high socks and a loose jersey looking like a pinup model but this considerate nigga ruined it. Me and Little Foot slowly turned to Ox with expressions of disgust and anger.

"You stole that from me, and I hate you for it," Thaxton whispered quietly.

"At least I got us all matching PJ's," he sighed while holding up three identical parcels. "That's cute right?"

"Shut up, Ox," we gruffed simultaneously.

Ox

They could be sour all they wanted, but these pajamas were cozy as fuck. I got all three of us some blue micro fleece polar bear PJs while Chrissy settled on a set covered in sketched bunnies.

Very fitting.

I had also struggled with a new duvet so we could all share a big blanket on the couch, which Blessing and Thaxton had reconfigured to make a sofa pit. Chrissy's head laid in my lap while the rest of her was stretched over the other two. Thaxton gently worked his fingers over her perfect feet with a eucalyptus massage oil while I scratched blue magic in between her braids. It was a perfectly normal and mundane set of actions but something about it was so magical.

Blessing could bitch about whatever, but this shit between us felt right.

"What do you guys want to watch?" Chrissy asked while flicking through streaming apps.

She started to boot up ESPN, but Thaxton calmly slid the remote out of her hand.

"It's bye week, Mamas. I don't want to hear no loud ass announcers or commentary until next Friday," he explained. "It's catch-up time."

Thaxton wasn't big on TV since he had a preference for reading, but Alex Cross had been on all of our lists for a month. He queued it up while Blessing made popcorn and I ordered a couple of pizzas for our inevitable midnight craving.

"This is an interesting combination," Chrissy smiled while nibbling at her second slice.

We were two episodes in when the pizza arrived. I got a classic cheese for the group, a meat lover's for Bless and L, with a chicken, jalapeno, bacon, and pineapple for myself. I knew the guys wouldn't fuck with it because they were sheep who thought pineapple on pizza was unholy, but Chrissy seemed to enjoy it.

"I discovered it while high out of my mind in undergrad," I confessed.

"That's how I discovered I liked boys," Blessing mumbled.

"I always knew," Thaxton added. "90s Brendan Fraser in The Mummy had me sick."

"That's gay," I chuckled while folding a slice into my mouth.

I was used to the playful shoves and the, "Shut up, Ox!" that followed. But Chrissy caught me off guard by reminding me of my earlier activities.

"Didn't you just cross swords with Thaxton in my coochie? I know you ain't talking," Chrissy giggled.

My mouth dropped open. No she didn't call me out on my bullshit. Who did she think she was, Bless?

"First off," I scoffed. "Fencing is an old world skill. An essential skill."

"Oh, is that right?" she smiled while scratching her nails through my beard.

Chrissy kept her nails short but they were meticulously groomed and shaped into a soft point that felt like heaven against my skin. I had to bite my lip to keep from drooling.

"Yesss," I hissed, slowly but surely forgetting my argument.

I saw L shake his head, casting his silent judgement on how quick I flipped for Chrissy. Then I remembered my second point.

"Plus I did that to make you cum. It's not gay to prioritize a woman's orgasm," I whispered while cupping her face.

And it usually wasn't. Truth be told I wanted to make her cum again right this second.

My dick twitched in my pants and Blessing must've been aware because he paused the show. Suddenly Chrissy's lips were on mine, her tongue invading my mouth while her ass was pressed firmly into Blessing's lap. He didn't seem to mind that much since he spread his legs to accommodate her, but L looked like he was going to implode.

"This is hot but I feel left out," he pouted.

"Come here," Chrissy cooed.

Thaxton scooted closer and she slipped her hand into his waistband and wrapped it around his dick. Then she did the same to me. All three of us groaned when she pumped us with those soft, capable hands. While Blessing looked like he was about to pass out when she ground against him to the same rhythm.

I took a break from her mouth to show some love to those pert nipples of hers that had been teasing me all night and Blessing took over her mouth for me with his middle and pointer finger. Chrissy's eyes traveled back and forth between what I was doing and Thaxton who was now making out with Blessing. Watching them suck each other's tongue while feeling up Chrissy made my dick harder than iron. It was the very definition of hedonistic and I wanted to get that shit memorialized in an oil painting. So maybe I was a little gay.

Or maybe it was just because Chrissy was so wet that she was leaking through the seat of her pj's. So wet that it looked like somebody turned on a faucet in her pants. Curiosity overwhelmed me and I eventually slid my palm down the front of her bottoms just to see how wet she really was and I was met with a slip n slide.
"Oh, Chrissy. This is ridiculous, princess," I sighed while rolling my thumb over her clit. "How is there even this much water in your body?"
"Because I was swallow," she moaned back with a lustful grin.
Yeah, Blessing had me fucked up. There was no way I was passing up the chance to make Chrissy mine. I didn't care who I had to share with. It being them just made the decision easier.

"You got a nasty little mouth," I grumbled before nibbling her neck.

She writhed against Blessing and he responded by cupping a handful of her ample bosom and flicking her nipples.

"I'm innocent," she protested with a pout.

"Yeah, I don't think so, Mamas," Thaxton laughed. "You take dick like a pro."

"Thaxton! Did you just call me a professional hoe?" she faux gasped.

"Yes," he nodded. "Nobody else could make three All-stars nut so hard they turn into putty. You're a real MVP."

"You're lucky I like shit like that," she laughed.

"We're lucky for a lot of reasons," Blessing moaned.

Suddenly he stood up with Chrissy in his arms and pulled down both her pants and his.

"I'm sorry, baby girl," he rasped while bracing her legs with his forearms. "I just can't take it anymore."

He plunged inside of her with one fluid thrust then me and Thaxton watched all the apprehension slowly bleed from his eyes. There were so many amazing things about Chrissy, but that pussy could make any non-believer a convert.

"Fuuuuccccckkkkk," he hissed while she rolled her hips against him.

I'm guessing that's when reality hit that nigga because he just dropped his head in defeat and tightened his grip around her waist. He was holding on for dear life, his muscles tense with restraint.

"Yeah, we probably should've warned you," Thaxton shrugged.

I disagreed because his demise was fun to watch, but sure.

"Warned him about what?" Chrissy sighed through their strokes.

"How addicting you are," I replied as L kneeled in front of them.

Thaxton pressed his lips to Chrissy's lower ones, sucking her hard clit into his mouth while Blessing fucked her deep and slow. She whimpered then cried, and I loved watching her head loll back from the assault of pleasure while her mouth hung open with a silent scream.

She was so blissed out.

What a perfect lil whore. Our perfect little whore.

Chrissy's creamy cum leaked down Blessing's dick and into L's mouth. Her wails ricocheted off the high ceilings while her glassy eyes were just one more stroke and hungry lick away from slamming shut.

"Please," she begged with a breathy moan.

The scene in front of me was sexy enough but then she just had to go and whimper. So in addition to stroking my own dick I now had a new task.

I was going to make her moan even louder.

Her bouncing breasts were heavy with need so I focused my attention there first. Licking, sucking, and kneading her soft, beckoning peaks. Chrissy had big ass titties and it made sense that her cocoa-colored areolas matched, but the size didn't stop me from trying to fit the entire thing into my mouth.

"Emmy," she grunted while collecting my locs in her fists. "Fuck, baby."

If my mouth wasn't full I would've asked her what time she wanted to go trade her car in tomorrow. Cause I was definitely putting my baby in a 2025 after this.

"More, more, more," she whined.

Her voice was raw and needy so Blessing didn't hesitate to give her just what she asked for. He threw his leg on the table and drilled her deep and quick while I sucked her tongue and L sucked her pussy. The loud claps from Blessing pounding her blended seamlessly with Chrissy's moans and her wet vac of a pussy, but then she stopped us with a request.

"Can you make me airtight?" she asked with a pout.

My train of thought derailed while I processed her request, but that's why I was lucky there were three of us. Thaxton didn't miss a beat. He hopped up ready to serve.

"How do you want us?" he smiled.

Eyes low and lips swollen, her gaze floated over the three of us until she solidified her plan.

This was her night after all.

"I want to taste you, Thax," she started. "I want Blessing to stay in my pussy and I want Emmy in my ass."

I gulped when I heard her request. Don't get me wrong my boys weren't lacking, but I was definitely the biggest.

Chrissy was a good foot shorter than me. Where was that foot going to go?

"Are you sure, princess? We can always try something else," I offered.

"I'm sure," she affirmed with a nod. "Besides, I know one of you has lube and I bet it's the good shit."

All three of us turned our heads toward Blessing, our resident bottom, with surety. To which he responded with a sigh before returning Chrissy to the couch.

"Let me go get that for you."

Blessing

I slid two fingers in and out of Chrissy's tight asshole until her back entrance was slick with lube then I coated Ox's dick with the other hand. I respected his boundary about not penetrating other guys, but I'd be lying if I said it wasn't disappointing sometimes. Outside of Little Foot, he had the most perfect dick I'd ever seen. Which is why I was mesmerized while watching Chrissy slide her ass down his heavy shaft.

"Oh fuck, fuck, fuck," she panted.

"Yeah that's the point," Ox chuckled while kissing her cheek. "You're getting fucked."

Her pussy puckered when they finally bottomed out and

couldn't help but give her swollen little clit a few endearing kisses. Those kisses turned into hungry sucks because she tasted so good, and I got to hear a few of Chrissy's sweet moans before L slid down her throat. I knew my snack time was over when I saw her impatient hand sneak towards her opening. So I waited just until she dipped her middle finger into her folds before giving Ox her hands and sliding back inside of her.

Chrissy felt amazing on her own, but the added tightness and the sensation of Ox moving inside of her was other-worldly. I was now starting to understand the appeal of sex parties. I probably would've nutted all over the place in any other situation, but luckily Chrissy had drained us hours earlier. I was less sensitive now and I was about to run her little ass ragged. I was seeking revenge.

How dare she waste this precious pussy on Derek's lame ass?

By the tenth stroke, her shit was so sticky it looked like my dick was tanghulu coated.

"Oh no. I'm cumming again," she whimpered.

"We know," Ox and I gruffed.

That wasn't news. Chrissy just kept cumming. Whether she decided to cream us or squirt was always a fun surprise, but her orgasms weren't. Ox pressed his palm against her lower belly then she tightened around us with a silent groan since she was also swallowing L. Her release was intense but not enough to milk us so we continued to torment her by plugging all three of her wet holes.

Right up until Little Foot withdrew from her mouth.

"I want some pussy too," he pouted. "Can you share a little bit?"

My first instinct was to say no because I'm a selfish asshole, but Chrissy's eyes glittered at the suggestion of us double filling her again. So I made space for him in between her legs.

"Yes," Thaxton exclaimed with a fist pump.

I had to admit his excitement was cute. Plus it made Chrissy smile.

"Don't do allat. I just want to remind you that I'm taking the lead here," I chided.

"Not a problem," L replied. "I'm just happy to be here."

"So am I," Chrissy giggled.

"And I'm one more laugh away from ruining everybody's night," Ox sighed while trying to hold Chrissy still.

"My bad," Little Foot grimaced. "I'm fucking up the flow."

I slung my arm over his shoulders and he did the same before we pressed our dicks together. I marveled at the differences between us as I gave our shafts a few pumps to get us nice and wet. Then once L's precum leaked out and mixed with mine, we eased inside of Chrissy.

"Shit, Mamas," Thaxton hissed.

My eyes rolled shut when we attempted our first stroke, as choppy and uncoordinated as it was. Thaxton was stiff and hot and Chrissy was wet and soft. It was the perfect juxtaposition. And so was her attitude.

"Open your eyes and look at me while you fuck me," she demanded while lacing her fingers around my neck.

I never encountered a power bottom before but it was a welcome surprise. It was cute that she was bossy while simultaneously being at my mercy. And I knew what she was asking was a bad idea, yet I still obeyed. When I cracked my eyes my vision immediately focused on her pussy and ass being stretched open by the three of us. Chrissy looked so fucking good all full, and hot, and soaking wet. She looked like she was ours. Those were dangerous thoughts to have at midnight.

"Baby girl, why do you feel so good?" I groaned.

I couldn't reach Chrissy's mouth from the angle I was at, so I sought Thaxton's instead to help guide me through the madness. It helped that he tasted just like Chrissy since he didn't bother to wash her out of his mouth from earlier, but I felt that tale-tell tingle in my spine when he wrapped my tongue in his and slid his tip along mine. I pulled away hoping to catch myself, but Chrissy's bottom lip ejected unexpectedly.

"What's wrong, baby girl?" I asked through our thrusts.

"I like watching you two kiss," she whined. "Why'd you stop?"

"Yeah, Blessing. Why'd you stop?" Thaxton moaned while driving my hips towards Chrissy with his free hand.

He knew good and damn well why I stopped. I stopped because we were ten seconds away from having to come up with some elaborate lie about us getting marshmallow fluff on the couch to appease Miss Yelena, and even then she wouldn't believe us.

Ox temporarily distracted Chrissy by taking her nipple into his mouth but she was still determined to get me back on track to blowing my load.

"Kiss him," she pleaded. "I know it feels good. It feels good to have you fuck me like this."

Around three months ago I had this random nagging theory that Chrissy wasn't always as proper and polished as she seemed and I was happy to know that I was correct. She was a Juilliard graduate, a lover of medium steak, a poetry collector, and also the freakiest woman I ever met.

I think I was in love.

"Chrissy feels good, doesn't she?" Thaxton moaned against my lips.

His teeth tugged at my quivering bottom lip as we fucked her deep and slow, pulling it into his mouth with a firm suck before pulling us apart so I could answer his question.

"S-so good," I shivered.

"Look at how pretty she is taking our dicks," he gritted while turning my chin.

I locked eyes with Chrissy and lost myself. Her chest heaved with soft, pleading moans. Her eyes were glassy with bliss, and her mouth was swollen from kisses and pleasure. She was a masterpiece and I knew there would never be another like her. She was one of a kind. One night had ruined me for good. I'd likely dream about this moment for years to come.

"You're so beautiful, Chrissy," I moaned while kissing her. My repositioning forced Thaxton to the outskirts of town, but he didn't seem to mind that one bit. I rambled off some hasty apology, but instead of his reply I heard the depression of the lube bottle pump twice before he pressed his middle finger to my asshole, and when I retracted from Chrissy he pushed into me. My stomach surged with rippling pleasure as I immediately exhaled with a strangled moan. Me and L had fucked plenty of times before but this was a first.
And also probably a bad idea.

Lucky Pierre's are one of those things you see and say, "I could definitely do that."
But when you actually find yourself sandwiched between giving and taking, two opposite ends of the spectrum, you realize why the world demonizes sexuality. Because knowing that this feeling was free was revolutionary. The world could probably heal if we all just fucked a little more.

"Jesus Devonte Christ, Bless," Ox hissed. "Why is your dick so hard? Is there any blood left in your brain?"
Honestly? There wasn't.
I was confident in my no too because I opened my mouth to talk and nothing came out. I would retreat from the luxuriating heat of Chrissy only for Thaxton to fuck me right back into her with his heavy dick. None of my

thoughts were coherent, not that they could've been because I could barely control my body. Instinct and pleasure were the only two driving forces in the room. I sought every last breath from Chrissy's mouth while I filled her perfect, fat pussy, Thaxton filled my ass, and Ox filled hers. The four of us rode that synchronized wave until I could no longer balance the load. Ecstasy bloomed deep in my belly and wrapped around my entire body. Then with an obnoxious, and truthfully embarrassingly, loud moan, I let the summation of my pleasure spill all in Chrissy.

It took too long for my breathing to even, and when it did I noticed that I had cracked the frame of the couch by grabbing it during my release. We spent six months looking for furniture that could handle the guaranteed abuse of seating three ten percentile athletes and I had invalidated all that hard work in just 30 minutes.
Chrissy was a public danger.

"So I take it you changed your mind?" Ox smiled as I stared at Chrissy.
L had long pulled out to grab a cleanup towel, but I was still firmly inside of her. Partly because I was afraid I would wake up and this dream would end if I moved, and partly because Chrissy felt like where I was always meant to be.
"Changed your mind about what?" she squeaked with those deep brown eyes shining up at me.
Her eyes were so big that I could see next Christmas in them clear as day. I could see pizza nights on our new

couch, cuddle puddles, and family ice-skating. I could even see our wedding day.

"Yeah I did," I nodded to Ox.

I pulled out of Chrissy and eased her off Emery before throwing her over my shoulder and heading upstairs.

"Cause we're keeping her."

I had the best sleep of my life that night. Sleep accented by deep relaxation and hazy pleasure. Chrissy would wake up to ride me, seeking me out with gentle, explorative touches, passionate kisses, and breathy moans. Then after she had taken me for what I was worth, she'd fuck Thaxton while sucking Ox. She graciously allowed us an hour of rest and then the cycle would repeat. It took two more rounds for her to get it all out of her system, and after all of that she collapsed between me and Ox, skin warm and damp with sweat, with Thaxton holding her hip while he spooned me. We had pushed two of the guest room's California Kings together so everyone could remain close and once Ox made it up with all those damn pillows and throws the bed was warm and cozy like a hibernation nest. Thaxton set the heat to something low and frosty so that we could enjoy the warmth of the night. I remember hearing Chrissy's snore competing with Ox's before thinking,

"Yeah, she'll definitely be out for a while."

I mean, who wouldn't be after a night like that?

So imagine my surprise when I woke up after a dreamless sleep and she wasn't in bed.

"What the fuck?" I hissed while searching the room. "Chrissy, baby?"

The light streaming in was golden and warm, alerting me to the possibility that we had slept well into the afternoon. With it being so late, Chrissy could've just been occupying a bathroom, but I was too impatient to wait and see if that was true. I threw Thax's heavy ass arm off of me and lept from the covers. However, I didn't give my body any time to fully acclimate to wakefulness, so it didn't surprise me when I stumbled out of bed and almost hit the wall. I barely pulled my core straight in time to avoid the TV and when I did, I almost doubled over again. My muscles screamed from overexertion, but I wanted to find Chrissy so I ignored it. Only for it to hit me on my second lap through the first floor.

I slid down the wall adjoining the kitchen with a pitiful grumble. Then I heard thunderous footsteps on the back stairs. Ox took one look at me and shook his head, sending his thick locks cascading across his shoulders.

"I'm gonna bring you a Powerade," he sighed with sleep still heavy on his voice.

I gave him a shaky thumbs up before slumping against the floor. That's all I could afford to do since my body was drained. Chrissy had literally fucked the shit out of me. I was appalled. Honestly though I should've known she was pressure from that split, but I had to have her anyway. Damn my persistence.

L took over my search for Chrissy after slipping back into PJs, searching both the recreation rooms and the outside courtyards before giving up.

"She's not here," he mumbled. "I-I think she ghosted us." I could hear the sting of rejection in his voice. Hell, I felt it too. As apprehensive as I was ten hours ago, I really did feel like there was something between us. Even when we were all just hanging out on the couch and discussing alien theories and teasing her and Ox for that travesty they considered pizza. For her to just up and leave without saying anything didn't make sense.

Several more beats of frustrated silence passed before we heard a cup clink against the kitchen counter.

"Oh shit," Ox grumbled as he flicked sleep out of his eyes. "Where y'all phones at?"

"What is it?" Thaxton exclaimed, eyes shining with hope. "Is it Chrissy?"

I too held out hope that she had sent us some kind of explanation, and technically I did get what I asked for.

Ox offered us his retina-burningly-bright screen which was hosting a post from the infamous gossip site Tea: Herbal Or Verbal? A post speculating about how the Minnesota Hare's beloved mascot was actually the team pass around.

"Are these pictures from the restaurant!?" Thaxton yelled.

They were, and while most of them were inconspicuous, the ones of me feeding her cake were suggestive at best. I say at best because you could definitely see the lust oozing from my gaze. It looked like I was seconds away from taking her down against the linens.

Then there was the one of us leaving with Ox palming her ass.

"Yes, and hella people are tagging Chrissy in the replies," Emery sighed. "It's been up for hours. I can't believe this was the first thing she saw."

Imagine having amazing, consenting sex with people who cared about you only for random Internet people to ruin it the next day. Imagine seeing a comment calling you a loose hoe at seven in the morning while the other participants caught no slack. Then imagine being alone with those feelings. I had no problem imagining the tears streaming down her cheeks, the hurt and confusion she must've felt, or the shame that was probably coiling in her belly.

Anger surged through me like a crackling thunderstorm, and I wanted to dismantle the world stone by stone for causing Chrissy pain. That felt more than reasonable. An eye for an eye, first born child for retribution type-shit. Some may say it was an overreaction, but I had waited so long to hold her and I knew there was no way I could give her up after just one night.

I was certain of that now.

"Ox, check the security cameras, L get in touch with that PR lady, and everybody get dressed," I gritted. "We're going to find her."

Chapter 4

Woman Hunt

Chrissy

Milly greeted me at the door with a cup of spiked hot chocolate with way too many marshmallows and a warm towel when I got out of my Muver. I made sure to tip the lady nicely, because after three attempts, she was the only driver who didn't ask whether or not Herbal Or Verbal was right about me getting dug out by the Minnesota Hares' star players last night. I'm sure she wanted to though. Her eyes were practically watering with curiosity.

I'll admit that I've indulged in a little celebrity gossip from time to time. Mostly because I thought it was just harmless speculation. A cute little hehe or some irrelevant clickbait at best. Now I knew that wasn't the case. My privacy was violated, and because I was in the public eye willingly, no one cared. My sex life was up for judgement just like everything else about me. Including my looks, my education, my upbringing, and my morals. They acted like I was Jeffrey fucking Dahmer instead of a horny woman who seized the day. Fucking was normal activity! It's not my fault that most people couldn't get more than one other person to join in.

"Hey cous," I huffed while stomping the snow off my boots. "Thanks for having me."
"Girl, please I needed the te-" Milly realized that she'd brought up that awful site and stopped with an awkward grimace before changing directions.
"I needed to check on you," she finished.
"Nice save. But I'll tell you everything," I waved. "I can smell Tristan's brownies from out here."

The air surrounding their house was perfumed with rich, salty butter, and quality chocolate. Milly's husband was obsessed with baking. There was always some sort of sweet treat around to nibble on regardless, but it was worse during the holidays. Two different cake stands sat half full on the coffee table and the dining room buffet, while Tristan carefully sliced into a fresh pan of brownies that were cooling on the rack. Milly often accused him of trying to keep her fat, but I think it was just another physical manifestation of his love for her. He indulged all of her varying interests, but especially her sweet tooth.

"Well, well, well, if it isn't the Hare's MVP," Tristan teased playfully. "Can I get you a brownie sundae?"

"Tris!" Milly chided with a pointed finger.

"It's ok," I sighed, waving Milly off. "I made my bed, I'm grown enough to lie in it."

My cousin dropped her head in between her shoulders with a loud sigh, sending her fluffy afro in multiple directions. At first I thought she was disappointed in me after hearing my confirmation of last night's alleged events, but it was just because her husband was an insatiable gossip.

"Oou I knew it! I told you she had her way with them!" Tristan exclaimed. "Let me get you another cup of cocoa and you can tell us all about it."

"Wait, wait, wait. You fucked them on the kitchen counter?" Milly gasped in awe.

I liked how that was the most scandalous part about my story in her eyes. Even though I had taken three dicks at once.

"It was marble," I laughed. "A nice light green color."

"Technically it was a kitchen island," Tristan corrected.

"Please keep up, Milani."

"Ope, not you using her full name."

"Yes, Christi–"

I stopped Tristan by launching a marshmallow at his face. As close as we were, my own mama didn't call me that and he wasn't about to either.

"Don't you dare!" I scolded. "That name is off limits."

"Your legal name is off limits?" he challenged while crossing his bony arms.

"Yes, just like your sexuality. Do you see me reminding Milly that she married a gay man?" I teased back.

"Not gay," he smiled. "Just bisexual like your boyfriends."

"Ope. He kinda ate you up there," Milly admitted, sucking her teeth.

And did.

It happened every time all of us got together. The three of us had grown up close with Tristan and his mom living across the street from our grandmother's house, but Tristan and Milly had always just clicked. You could tell very early on that they would end up together, and the relationship that blossomed between them during adolescence and young adulthood surprised no one. Not even Milly's father, Uncle Milton, who had lots of opinions about everything, including Tristan's sexuality. Even he couldn't deny that Tris adored Milly.

Which is why I couldn't stand it at times.

I wanted that kind of undeniable, effortless love too. I almost thought I could have last night truth be told, but that might've just been a Mighty Minnesota Hares induced pipe-dream.

Speaking of which...

"Ugh, don't call them that. It was nice for a night, but I promise the state's most eligible bachelors are not checking for me. They got what they wanted and so did I," I gruffed.

Tristan jerked his head back, physically appalled by my statement. Then he turned to his wife with a skeptical eyebrow raised high.

"Didn't you tell me the center had been pursuing her from the jump?" Tris questioned.

"Mhm," Milly confirmed with a nod. "He flooded the women's locker room with daisies for her birthday. He also catered a dinner buffet for her since she had to work. From Caparadelli's Pasta Company *and* Naan Factor. That's where she brought us those plates from."

Tristan brought his fist to the edge of his teeth with a grimace. I stilled in my seat, dreading whatever tongue-lashing was going to come my way. Because one thing about Tristan, he didn't believe in letting people live in their delusion. He was a realist 100%.

"Chrissy, Imma keep it a buck," he started.

"Alright," I nodded.

"If you don't marry that man, me and Milly will," he finished.

"Tris!" I protested. "I- It's not like that!"

What happened between us was just sex. Sure, Blessing was sweet and attentive at times, most times if I'm being honest, but I'm sure it was just means to an end. He already told me we weren't friends.

"Ok, but it really is," he scoffed. "Men are simple creatures that pursue what they want. I know that because I am one. When's the last time Derek bought you a bouquet, let alone several?"

My shoulders slumped because we all knew the answer was never. I had accepted the bare-fucking-minimum from that bum.

"Clock it," Milly cheered from the sidelines.

"Mil," I sighed.

"I'm not trying to make you feel bad," Tristan said gently. "But I want you to know that he's pursuing more than just sex. That kind of effort is usually reserved for a relationship. He likes you, Chrissy."

"Ok, but what about the other two? Em bought me a whole ass department store worth of pj's that were all in my favorite color, then Thaxton literally washed my back and planned a last minute trip to Chicago. So what, I'm just supposed to pick one and forget that I also have feelings for the others?" I argued.

"What if you just don't pick?" Milly shrugged. "It's not like they asked you to."

"Yeah I tried that and now Kevin Samuel's Legion Of Goochlickers are calling me a high-mileage hoe," I chuckled derisively.

"Who cares about what some broke ass incel thinks? You have three men with big bags who are interested in you. Monogamy isn't automatically better than polyamory, it's just different. Different people love in different ways and that's ok."

Her words hit me in the chest like a two piece.

"You know, I hate when you use your insightfulness against me," I pouted.

"No one is safe," Milly chuckled. "But seriously, promise me you'll think about it?"

"Yes, yes," I sighed in agreement. "I will seriously consider living up to my high-mileage hoe reputation. Just as soon as I find out if I still have a job."

The team manager and Coach Vickers had been calling me all morning, but I had put my phone on DND hours ago after the onslaught of tags on Instagram and Bluesky. I figured I'd deal with it later, and later had come.

"What do you mean, find out if you still have a job?" Tristan scoffed.

"Well my contract has a morality clause, and lots of people think having a train ran on you is immoral," I shrugged.

"That hasn't been publicly confirmed," Milly argued. "And you really should start letting Tris look at your contracts beforehand."

"I will next time," I nodded. "But right now, can I get a ride to my car?"

"Yeah I got you," Tris confirmed. "I need to get some bread flour anyway."

Milly rolled her eyes while taking a big bite of what I suspected to be her second brownie. The dark chocolate spread across her wide lips as she threw in a faux snarl for effect. She pretended to be upset, but her dramatics were a front so she didn't catch too much flack from our aunties for her annual holiday weight gain. And Tris knew it too.

"Also, Mills," I started, distracting her from lecturing Tristan. "I need to borrow a wig."

Ox

After checking the cameras, we discovered that Chrissy slipped into a Muver through the backdoor three hours before we'd woken up. She literally stumbled out of the house, looking every bit as stiff and exhausted as she likely felt. Her thick braids were thrown up high into a loose bun while the rest of her head and neck was wrapped in one of my scarves that barely showed her sleepy, swollen features. She looked like she was in a hurry, but funny enough she still stopped long enough to tend to one of the hellebores on the back patio with a bottle of water. Our sweet girl.

"Her car isn't here," Blessing huffed. "We must've just missed her."

Correction..

Our quick, sweet girl.

Figuring she wouldn't be able to get far without reliable transportation, we called in a favor to stadium security to check if her car was still where we left it. It was, so we all piled in L's truck and sped up 94 to try and catch her. Unfortunately for us though, the thirty minute commute was all the time she needed to shake our trail. She wasn't answering our calls and texts either. So we were now in need of a backup plan. Given the alternatives, I began to wonder if it was too cloudy to deploy a helicopter for our search...

"I really hate to bring this up, but did you ask Liam if he's seen her?" I sighed.

Liam Honsen was the team's manager and also a personified hemorrhoid. Irritating, red, and concerningly swollen. We didn't agree on much as an entire team, but we could all agree that Liam had the personality of a cheese grater. Luckily for him though, he was extremely proficient at his job. Which made him "indispensable" to the league and the team's owners. I personally hoped he stubbed his big toe every morning, but today I'd have to tuck that disdain into my back pocket in hopes of finding Chrissy.

Wherever she had gone.

Me and Blessing exchanged looks, silently pressuring each other to volunteer. But before we could set our sights on L, he excused himself as an option.

"Don't look at me," Thaxton chuckled. "Cause I'm in a fighting mood."

Damn.

Honestly that left just me.

Bless was neurotic, bordering on unhinged from trying to find Chrissy and get all of the articles taken down, and as funny as the proposition was, I knew I couldn't let Little Foot get his rounds in with Liam. Thax really was in a fighting mood and was also probably one misplaced comment from finding out how Craig got fired on his day off.

"Damnit, I'm going," I gruffed.

The other two fell behind me and we shuffled up to management's offices in a single file line. Before we could reach the door at the end of the hall, however, we ran right into Liam.

"Well, well, well. If it isn't the three stooges. I was hoping to catch you," he sneered, voice nasally and dry.

"Excuse me?" I scoffed.

We'd heard it all before. The Three Amigos, The Three Musketeers, The Three Stooges. That wasn't the problem. It was his tone that was killing me. Liam spoke to us like we were wayward kids instead of three grown ass men whose performance paid his bills.

"Don't get your panties in a bunch, Ox. It's not necessary. Not after the mess you've all made."

I raised my hand slowly, subconsciously cupping it into the width of Liam's neck. Part of me knew I couldn't choke out the team's manager, but I allowed myself to dream for that split second between steadying breaths. Luckily, Blessing stepped in to prevent that dream from becoming a reality.

"Listen, Liam. We're just wondering if you've seen Chrissy today," he sighed. "We're worried about her."

Liam rolled his eyes at Blessing's inquiry, and me and Thaxton were practically foaming at the mouth by the time his reply came.

"No I haven't seen your little friend, but if you see her before I do, tell her to start looking for employment elsewhere. She's fired."

Little Foot, who was previously behind me, immediately pushed his way to the front, damn near knocking my big ass over.

"Fired? Fired for what?" he hissed.

It seems like common sense surged through Liam briefly as he swallowed whatever smart-ass comment he originally had and gave Thaxton a straight answer.

"She violated her morality clause," Liam mumbled. "The Hares' run a family business. We can't have our mascot publicly participating in orgies. It's against contract."

"See, here's the thing. As far as we're concerned, that's speculation. Ain't nobody physically see any of us do shit "compromising," he gritted, his voice heavy with tension. "And speaking of contracts, mine is about to be up for renewal. It'd be a shame if the Hares' lost their best winger over a misunderstanding. I hear New York is beautiful this time of year."

L could've been bluffing, but I had a strong suspicion that he wasn't based on the way he acted when he found out Chrissy had left that morning. Liam didn't know that though. What he did know, however, was that New York, Chicago, and even Toronto had expressed increased interest in L throughout the years. Come to think of it, they'd tried to scalp all of us at one point or another. Not to toot our own horn, but we were that good.

"I like New York," I added. "They got some good ass food. Best Jollof outside of Nigeria."

"I've always wanted to do Christmas in Times Square," Blessing chuckled. "It's so magical."

Having to replace three players immediately after the Stanley Cup would be a nightmare, having to replace three of your best players though? Anxiety paled the normally tomato-red man to a Casper-ish hue. I try not to be problematic unlike some of us, but even I had to admit that shit was hella funny. Liam deserved to be taken down a notch.

"Is this a threat?" Liam murmured while choking down a swallow.

"No, but it is a possibility. Look, she's out there busting her ass every week, same as us. Like it or not, Christine is part of our team and we'll happily take one for the team," I replied.

I'm sure we were really living up to the Three Musketeers namesake now, but that was fine because it was working. Liam's agonizingly tight shoulders dropped in defeat when he released a conceding sigh.

"Look, I'd love to just forget about this, but the articles-"

"What articles?" Blessing smiled.

Liam cocked his head to the side, probably silently questioning if Bless had any recent head trauma, before pulling out his phone. His bushy, unkempt brows began to merge as he scrolled and swiped, searching for whatever gossip rags he'd originally seen us plastered all over, but they were all gone.

L was right about having a personal PR team. They were worth every penny.

"Well, gentlemen," Liam chuckled with a nervous gulp. "It appears I have some phone calls to make."

He ran his weathered hand through his dishwater-colored hair while scrolling one more time for good measure before retreating back into his little goblin lair.

"You do that," L sneered. "And please be sure to send the owner, whose ass you suck, my regards, shit stain!"

I sucked in my stomach to withhold my laugh while Blessing doubled over shamelessly. I didn't want to encourage L's bullshit but he made it so goddamn hard. Civility just wasn't in his vocabulary. Especially not when it came to Liam.

"Go to hell, Thaxton!" he yelled back while closing the door.

Luckily, Liam was used to it though.

"Everyday I have to interact with you is hell enough, superstar!" L hollered while blowing a kiss down the hall.

He rolled his shoulders backwards to free the tension that accumulated from their conversation before facing us with a grin.

"Well, what now?" Blessing asked.

"Not gone lie, I was thinking about a helicopter search," L shrugged.

"Yoooo, same," I said, throwing my head back. "It'd make this shit so much easier."

"This is exactly what I was talking about last night," Bless grumbled. "You two idiots are going to blow up this woman's life, and she'll want nothing to do with me by default."

I clutched my figurative pearls, the ones I inherited from Granny Pam, and gasped, raising the pitch of my voice for dramatics. It got a laugh out of Thaxton, which is why he was my favorite.

"How selfish of you!" I declared.

"Yeah, like getting a helicopter to find a traumatized lady isn't," Bless tutted. "Come on Tweedle-Dee and Tweedle-Dum. There's one more place we can check."

Me and Thax joined hands and swung them cheerfully. It pissed Blessing off and he scowled at us.

"Don't be cute," he hissed as L started the truck. "We got a missing woman to find."

Blessing

"Yeah, she's not here."

I took a step back from the porch stoop to check the house number. 1616 Perry Lane, the exact address I dropped her off at six months ago when Devon "borrowed" Chrissy's car and "forgot" what time the game ended. I offered to take her straight home despite it being in the opposite direction of where I was headed, but she insisted here was fine because she needed to blow off steam. I watched her climb out of my Mercedes, shoulders heavy with disappointment and tight with frustration. It was summer so her natural curls were fluffy and free having just been washed after enduring the hell of her dancing in that zoot suit for 90 minutes.

Then her skin, which was practically radiating from the day's leftover sunlight, shined under the same bronze and black porch sconce I was standing next to.
This was definitely the right house.

"Um, but you are Milly, right?" I asked.
"Yes, but for future reference, it's rude to pop up at people's homes without being explicitly invited, Mister Hockey Man," she chided.
I knew that, and if my Mama knew that I was currently disregarding that lesson, she'd have my hide. Yet I continued to act like Angel Harrel didn't give me any home training.
Because I was desperate.

"I'm sorry," I said, hanging my head in shame. "I'm just worried. She left this morning without saying anything, then all the articles and post, and-"
I trailed off, realizing I might be saying too much, but Milly didn't let me wonder about that for long. She gave me a coy smile that silently commended my effort before turning me loose for good.
"You know, I like that you're checking on her, but she's really not here. She stopped by at 11 and then my husband dropped her off at her car. I have no idea where she is, and believe me, I wish I did. She has my good wig and it's date night."

I was about to ask if there was a possibility that the aforementioned husband knew Chrissy's whereabouts, but before I could, a silver work truck with dark tinted windows rolled into the driveway. A man no smaller than 6'3 hopped out, stomping across the gravel, fully ready to whoop my ass if I was causing trouble for the woman at the door. A white gold wedding band contrasted against the reddish-brown hue of his skin, declaring him Milly's husband. That made me realize that the Hawkins' women had a type. Big, brawny, and protective. A standard me and the guys met thrice.

"Everything alright?" he asked, his voice tense with warning.

I could tell he was warning me to get the fuck off his property. Honestly, I couldn't blame him. If three random-ass men were on my porch, questioning my wife, I'd have a problem too.

"Everything's fine, Tris," Milly giggled. "They're looking for Chrissy. Did she tell you where she was going?"

The man's eyes narrowed, blocking out some of the winter sun so he could focus on my features. Then he glanced over his shoulder to Ox who gave a friendly wave from the passenger seat of the truck. His expression softened instantly, and he shot his wife a conspiring smile.

"Oh shit, it's the Hares. My bad I didn't recognize you at first," he explained before offering me an impressively firm handshake. "I'm not much of a sports guy."

"It's alright," I shrugged, taking his extended palm.

My brother also wasn't a sports guy, which is why he'd only been to three of my games since I started in the league. So I could understand. Plus I was relieved and slightly humbled to find the limitations of my fame.

"I don't mean to impose, or be rude, I- We just wanted to find Chrissy," I explained, motioning my head towards the other two.

Tris grimaced as he released my hand, tucking it into his back pocket to fetch his phone.

"Oof, that's gonna be a hard one. I don't know where she went either. I dropped her back at her car almost two hours ago," he clicked.

I threw my shoulders down in a fit of frustration. It was almost dinner time and we still couldn't find her. We'd spent hours driving around the city, examining every little breadcrumb she left to no avail. We were basically chasing a wild rabbit.

"Damn, and she didn't say anything?"

"No, not really," Tris said with a head shake. "All she said was she needed some good air. Whatever the fuck that means."

The few bits of sugar leftover from the morning's Powerade flew straight to my brain to ignite the lightbulb that had been aimlessly rattling around in there.

"Thank you!" I exclaimed, racing back to the truck. "I owe you one!"

"Please be careful saying that," Milly warned. "Everyone isn't humble like Chrissy."

I couldn't reply because I was busy throwing the truck in drive so we could go get our girl, but I would have replied, "I know."

Because there was no one in the world quite like Chrissy. And that's why we were going to make her ours.

Chapter 5

Magic

C hrissy

The frigid air nipped at my exposed ears and chin since the warmth of the winter sun had waned. I had been sitting at the dock of Pickerel lake for hours, hoping to get some of the good air that surrounded the place when the northern lights came out to play. It was getting late though, and I knew I didn't have much longer to continue ignoring my protesting stomach without suffering some kind of consequence. Still I hugged my legs tighter to my chest. I needed more time to sort everything out. My job, my family, my *relationships*, if you could even call them that. I was overwhelmed, too overwhelmed to even think of managing dinner, and definitely too overwhelmed to head back into the city, where someone would recognize me as the Hares' All-Hole-Hoe.

It wasn't exactly slut-shaming, because I was a grown ass woman who didn't feel shame for having consenting sex that resulted in the best nut of my life. It was more like heckling, and heckling got tiresome quickly. I still didn't regret it.

No, I'd never regret it.

But times like this made me wish I had a fairy godmother to swish her magic wand and clean up this big ugly mess so that I could unwind with a midnight bubble bath and a cheery birdsong. I wanted my glass chariot to turn back into a pumpkin, at least for a little while.

Unfortunately all of the stars in the sky tonight were stationary, so I knew there was no way for my wish to come true. Magic or otherwise. So maybe I'd wait out the crowd a little longer and enjoy the northern lights instead. It had been years since I had the time to do that.

I tilted my chin heavenward, silently asking for a sign that everything was going to work out, only to hear a faint, "Chrissy," a little while later.

I looked around for signs of other visitors, but I was alone. No lights, no cars, no camping tents. So either I had nutted so hard that it had caused brain damage or the sky was talking to me.

"Mkay Miss Universe, what happened to moving in mysterious ways?" I questioned.

Silence returned to me only to disappear again with another,

"Chrissy!"

This time growing closer and more urgent. It sounded kind of like Ox.

I saw undefined shadows slinking toward me. They were moving fast so I scrambled to my feet just in case I had to run, but a few feet later, I realized it was actually Ox, with Blessing, and Thaxton. Trudging up the hill with the same indescribable determination I saw them carry on game days.

"What are you guys doing here?" I shrieked. "How did you even find me?"

"Blessing," Ox supplied sunnily. "We stopped by your cousin's house-"

My eyes nearly popped out of my head. For all the explanations in the world I expected, that wasn't one of them. I honestly would've believed that they found me via helicopter before that.

"You stopped by my cousin's house?"

"Wait, let me explain," Bless said, racing to the front of the line.

"Explain."

"Ok, well. You left before we woke up. So I went looking for you at your cousin's. Her husband said you went to go get some good air. I remember you mentioned coming to Pickerel lake when you feel sad because the northern lights made the air magic. So I figured you came here."

"I did."

"We saw the articles."

"Ok."

"We got them all removed."

My expression relaxed and then my posture followed. I definitely didn't expect that.

When my shoulders finally dropped I used the momentum to retrieve my phone from my back pocket. Lo and behold, everything was gone. Every post, article, comment, and meme. It was like they never existed in the first place. Like last night never happened.

Although I had the soreness and fuzzy socks to prove it definitely did.

"How did you do this?" I gasped.

"I got a cutthroat PR lady," Thax beamed. "The best in the business."

 For a second I thought actual magic was involved but that made sense. Sometimes I forgot that the guys had big money and crazy connections. This was a nice reminder.

"Thank you," I nodded with fat tears streaming down my face.

"No problem," Ox said, stepping closer. "Also, you're not fired."

Now that was for sure the direct result of magic. 29 missed calls from Liam and I wasn't fired? It's a Christmas miracle, Charlie Brown.

"Thanks for that too, although I should probably quit anyway," I shrugged.

"Why?" Thaxton scoffed. "You love your job."

"Yeah, I do. But that doesn't change the fact that everyone

now knows we fucked. I'll get harassed."

"Did you know that a hockey stick doubles as a weapon?" Thax asked, unblinking. "Plus we have Ox."

"Hey, I'm a lover," Ox protested.

"You're a tank," Thaxton scoffed.

Ox shrugged.

I got the distinct impression that Thaxton Paul would happily commit murder if it came down to it. Oddly, I didn't disapprove.

"You can't fight every time someone bothers me, Thax," I sighed.

"But I could."

"Shut up," Blessing hissed. "You're fucking this up for us."

He turned to me with adoration and something akin to hope in his eyes.

"Look, Chrissy. What the guys are trying to say-"

"Mostly Little Foot," Ox interjected.

"What mostly L is trying to say," Blessing nodded. "Is that we got you. We aren't gonna stand by and let people abuse you."

"I appreciate that," I nodded.

I didn't make any attempts to move towards them or soften my defenses. The ornery wind whipped around us, making me wish I could, but this was still just too compli-cated. It was too uncertain. I had just spent a year dealing with uncertainty and I didn't want to do that again. I think they knew that though because their shoulders fell in defeat.

"Christine," Emery said after a while, command evident in his tone. "Come here."

My full name was off limits. I hated being referred to as Christine. This was a fact. And yet for reasons I couldn't readily explain, my feet shuffled forward. I got just close enough and Ox slipped his arms around my waist, pulling me into their warm little huddle.

"Listen, what these two are trying to say is that we like you, we'll protect you, and that you don't need to quit your fucking job because you're the best mascot the Hares have ever had, and as much as I dislike conflict, I will beat a muhfuckas head in for harassing you."

"Em," I sighed, while tilting my head upwards to stare into his hazy brown eyes. "All of that sounds great in theory, but there is no uncomplicated way to navigate this between us."

"So what?" he shrugged. "Everything is complicated. The economy is chaos, the world's on fire, the government is a shitshow. Just let us love on you."

He kissed my cheek with those soft, full lips of his and my knees almost buckled when his locs brushed against my collar. But I knew I wouldn't fall because I was surrounded on all sides. As much as it pained me to admit it, it felt right. It felt safe.

"You make it sound so easy," I mumbled.

"Yeah, because it is," Blessing replied. "Being with you is very easy. For all of us."

His gaze flitted over Ox and Thaxton briefly before returning to me.

"Honestly Chrissy, I have never wanted someone as bad as I want you. You're witty, kind, and tenacious. I told you I wasn't your friend last night because I don't wanna be. I much rather be your man. Or at least one of them. Women like you rule the world and everything in it. It's not fair but there's nothing I can do about it, and I know it wouldn't be fair to make you choose either. So can we all just take the easy way out and be a team?"

"Are you asking me to be the team girlfriend?" I chuckled.

"Not the whole team," Thax interjected. "Just ours. The three of us. Is that alright?"

Could I enjoy pizza on the couch during bye weeks and off seasons, snuggle up and binge-watch TV, and have riveting conversations about whether or not we were in a simulation? Could I fall asleep in their arms and feel weightless most nights? Would that be alright? I brought my pointer finger to my chin in thought, pretending to seriously consider any other answer but,

"Ok. I'll be your pass around."

"Girl hush," Ox said, patting my little booty.

I chuckled as the boys made a circle around me, squeezing me tight and peppering me in kisses.

"I can't believe I thought about giving this up ten minutes ago," I giggled as Blessing's lips tickled my ears.

"I would've changed your mind," he whispered. "Me and L would've broken into your car and left flowers everywhere and Ox would've left a really sweet apology note. You might've ended up calling the police but I'm sure you would've swooned for a split second."

"It's concerning that you know that and remain unapologetic," I chuckled.

"It's concerning how much I like you," he shrugged while kissing my temple.

"You know what else is concerning?" Ox said, breaking our huddle. "The fact that we're standing here in the dark when we could be getting dinner."

"That is concerning," I conceded with a nod.

My stomach gurgled and with that, I was slung over Em's shoulder to be carried back down the hill.

"What are you doing for New Year's?" Thaxton asked.

"Getting a squatter removed," I answered, remembering Derek.

"Don't worry about that. I've already handled it. What are you doing for the countdown?"

"Surprisingly, after getting my business outed, I don't have plans."

"Well now you do."

"Ok, now I do," I smiled.

The rest of the journey back to the parking lot was quiet, highlighted by the sounds of Em stomping through the crunchy, frozen snow and the harsh whipping of the winter winds. I probably would've been freezing if I took this walk alone, but instead I was warm and comfortable.

"Guys?" I squeaked. "Thanks for coming to get me."

"Of course, baby," Em grunted. "We meant it when we said you were ours."

His hand came to the middle of my back, quieting my

racing mind. We still had a lot to figure out and I was certain it'd be difficult sooner rather than later. However when I looked up I saw the northern lights dancing across the evening sky. Magic raced down my spine, real as ever. And I knew I had found a good thing with the Mighty Minnesota Hares.

Epilogue
New Year's Eve 2025: Blessing

"**A**nd best dressed for 2025 goes to…. Thaxton Paul!" Ox announced.

Three months ago, Chrissy had the idea for us to have a family award show. I was on board simply because it made her happy, but this was the funniest shit I'd ever done in my life. We dressed in suits and Chrissy put on her Sunday's best so we could enjoy a catered dinner from the comfort of our living room. We all voted for each other in various categories including best dressed, best recipe, best vacation idea, and best cuddler. Of course Chrissy unanimously won best cuddler. I loved the guys and I knew they loved me but no one could compete with a soft, brown sugar babe with warm pillows on her chest. T

haxton gave a dramatic acceptance speech, thanking everyone from his Mama, to Milly, and even his number-one hater Liam, but especially Chrissy.

"And in conclusion, I'd like to say that you niggas should try harder next year," he laughed. "Except for you, Chrissy. You're perfect, baby."

Me and Ox rolled our eyes simultaneously as L added to his unnecessary antics with a deep bow before scooping Chrissy up for a kiss. He was lucky she reciprocated, because if she hadn't me and Ox would've tripped him.

"Aight, sit down," Ox grumbled. "We got one more category."

"One more category?" Chrissy exclaimed. "Wait, I only voted for six. I thought this was it."

Confusion inked her expression as she fought to recount the evening after what I'm pretty sure was her fourth drink. Technically she was right. There were originally six categories, but me and the guys added a last-minute revision to the ballot. Not that we needed to vote, because it was another unanimous decision.

"The final Fammy of the night, for the best live-in girlfriend goes to," Ox trailed while opening his envelope. "CHRISTINE HAWKINS!"

Me and L launched confetti into the sky while blowing our shitty paper party whistles. It rained down on

Chrissy, landing in her pretty, pinned-up curls like fresh snow.

"Aw, you guys. That was really sweet," Chrissy cooed as she accepted her award.

It took her a minute to notice the keys hanging off the statue, but when she did her mouth fell open with a gasp.

"Wait, did you say live-in?"

"Yes we did, baby girl," Ox chuckled. "If it's ok with you, we'd like you to move in and takeover. We like having you here."

"Yeah, that independent woman living in the big city shit is cute, but you should be coming home to a hot meal every night," L added.

"Thaxton, stop talking before I smother you with a pillow," I grunted. "You're going to fuck this up."

"First off, do not smother anyone with the pillows I just picked out," Chrissy admonished with a pointed finger. "And second, off. You guys don't have to convince me. I actually like my boyfriends."

"Oh thank God," I faux-sighed. "I thought you were just in this for our massive dicks and accompanying bank accounts."

"Who said I wasn't?" she teased.

Ox walked over and scooped her off the couch with a playful grimace that would be terrifying if it was aimed at anyone else.

"I keep telling you that mouth is gonna get you in trouble," he growled while lightly shaking her.

"I think it already has," she chuckled. "Cause now I gotta explain to my daddy why I'm sharing a bed with three other guys."

"Chrissy, Mr. Dennis knows we fuck," L snorted.

After four months, we had sat everyone's family down to explain the situation. Surprisingly no one acted a complete ass, but we did get the occasional odd look. Media didn't bother us much if at all though, and I suspect that's because L's crazy ass threatened the local paps. Regardless, Chrissy's parents were 100% on board. I suspect that's because she's an only child, a perpetual good girl, and we took care of her. So if they were initially upset, it didn't last for long.

"No," she corrected. "He knows we're dating."

"Sure, and that hickey on your neck came from a doorknob," L smiled. "Get ready y'all. The countdown is starting."

Ox returned Chrissy back to the center of the sofa and we all huddled close with champagne in hand, counting down backwards to a new year full of opportunity, growth, and memories to be made.

"Five, four, three, two, one! Happy New Year!" we cheered.

I kissed Ox first, then L, and finally Chrissy. While my boys were sweet pecks, locking lips with Chrissy was anything but. Her tongue probed gently and I deepened our kiss, sucking her in like I was a man who had gone without. I heard L and Ox sigh while we went at it and I knew I would never hear the end of it for ruining our plan, but I truly couldn't help it.

"Anyway," Ox said, while raising his glass. "To new experiences."

"To new experiences!" Chrissy cheered while rushing to join in on the toast.

Our glasses clinked together merrily, with golden champagne swishing ever so slightly over the rim before we brought them back to our mouths.

"And speaking of new experiences," L smiled. "We got you something, Mamas."

Ox handed Chrissy a large box with a big pink bow. She smiled before shaking it to try and figure out what it was and I got happy all over. Christmas gifts were nice, but we wanted to start our own traditions. Chrissy gave up looking for a hint and slowly pulled the ribbon connecting the bow until the lid loosened. She slid her hand inside but when she couldn't determine what it was, she tore the box apart like a little tornado.

"Is this baby oil?" she asked, lifting four bottles into her arms.

It was baby oil gel, to be specific.

"Yes, because we want you to experience everything you didn't last year," I explained.

She cocked her head onto her shoulder, letting those gorgeous, brown eyes burrow into me while she considered my words. Only to give up with a shrug.

"I don't understand," she admitted.

"Well," Ox chuckled, his voice deepening. "Do you remember when you said you wanted us to get greasy like old-school Pizza Hut and fuck the shit out of you?"

Her eyes widened while her lip came between her teeth. She definitely remembered, even if she was trying to play it off with that little innocent smirk.

"We remember," L replied. "We were on the beach in Bangkok and you had on that little orange two piece. You were drunk off Mai Tai's and rum punch when you said it, but we knew you were serious because your pussy got wet when you told us."

We all inched closer, caging her in so that she had nowhere to run when she tried to deny it. She had shown us her hand on the first night and we knew what she was capable of. Which is why it surprised us all when she said,

"I hope we don't fuck up the leather. Get naked, boys."

I took one look at her before loosening my belt and then helping Ox with his.

"Christine, we love yo nasty ass," I sighed.

"I know, and I love you too," she smiled. "Now help me out of this dress. We got memories and messes to make."

I found myself questioning if I was mentally well after thinking about all the things I wanted to do to them, but I still didn't hesitate to get naked because they were waiting on me and I'd happily take one for the team any day of the week.

The end

Thank you!

Thank you so much for taking the time to read One For The Team in all it's glorious chaos. If you have the time, please consider leaving me a review. Reviews not only help me grow as a writer, but they also help other readers like you find my work and get a shot at seeing themselves represented in romance. Again, thank you for giving me your time and support, and as always, I hope to see you in the next story!

About the author

Aria is a die-hard romantic and her main goal is to always be drying her eyes from something sickly sweet. She has been dreaming up romance stories since she was seven years old, with the first one being a Toy Story fanfic. She's also a Neo-soul and R&B enthusiast who's forever got a song stuck in her head. You can find her looking for good food, reading, writing, or enjoying time with her family in her free time. She lives happily in Saint Louis, Missouri with her middle school sweetheart-turned-husband and their adorably chaotic son. Her dream is to one day write inclusive stories that center BIPOC full-time, but for now, she labors in fraud as a working stay-at-home mom.

Also by Aria

Glory
https://www.amazon.com/dp/B0D1YH9BNH
Burry The Hatchette
https://www.amazon.com/dp/B0CT34SSS4
Candy Corn Curses
https://www.amazon.com/dp/B0DJLQ3W14
Rudy Jones's New Year's Resolution
https://www.amazon.com/dp/B0CLMWNPQJ
From Kingston, With Love
https://www.amazon.com/dp/B0CPDFXY9P
Bloom
https://www.amazon.com/dp/B0C82QWN2F
Candid
https://www.amazon.com/dp/B0BZMZVZ47
Human Resources
https://www.amazon.com/dp/B0DMR5NY9X

You May Also Like

Looking for more Why Choose Romances? Check out some of my favorites!

Just Right-Shon

Seeing Red-Shon

The Air Between Us-Shameka S. Erby

All I Want For Christmas Is Two -Shameka S. Erby

Crave-Shae Sanders

Who You Belong To- ML Bash

WitchTrapment- ML Bash

Sweet Heat- Lady Marie

Fated Frenzy- Gigi Zarbi

All I Want For Christmas- Lily S. Flowers

Hurry Down My Chimney Tonight- Lily S. Flowers

The Oath- T.M. Richardson

The Offer- T.M. Richardson